DEDICATION

THIS BOOK IS DEDICATED TO MY FRIEND AND COLLABORATOR PATRICIA WESTON OF CORNWALL WHOSE IDEA LED TO THE CREATION OF THE STORY.

I OFFER MY GRATEFUL THANKS TO MY SON, STEPHEN, WHO DESIGNED THE COVER AND TO MY WIFE FRANCES FOR GIVING HER TIME AS EDITOR.

MAIDSTONE KENT

1st JUNE 2020

Copyright ©2020 Norman McGill

All rights reserved.

ISBN: 9798652889081

In friendship

Norman

LIST OF CHARACTERS AND OTHER REFERENCES

THE GODS & GODDESSES

Thor -King of the Gods

Odin-of thunder, strength and determination.

Frigg – of love and marriage. Wife of Odin

Freya-known as "The lady"; of love and fertility.

Sjofn-of harmony and human love

Aegir- of the sea

Ran -of the sea; partner of Aegir. Both practical jokers.

Loki-joker and trouble maker

Baldur-of peace

NARVIC

FRODE

His parents - Eric and Helga

His sisters– Jora, Katla, Runa.

FREYA

Her parents - Gustav and Ranveya

Her brother-Harid

Her sister- Inga

THE CHILDREN

Frode, Freya, Gustav, Hortha, Lodi, Inga, Magaretha

FREYA'S BUSINESS TEAM

Margaretha, Harid, Runa, Olaf

HJALTLAND (THE SHETLAND ISLANDS)

Bjorn-head of family Frode visits

Fiona-friend of Bjorn's family -becomes fond of Frode

DYFLIN (DUBLIN)

Caolinn, landlord's daughter

Ronan-monk from Glendalough Monastery

Peter, the monk teaching Frode languages

KILKENNY (IRELAND) Viking unnamed

Niall and Clodagh-local farmers

VEORAFJOROR (WATERFORD, IRELAND)

Cathal-leader of the group of people living in Waterford

Peter- local story teller-befriends Frode.

Connel and Kathleen- child storytellers coached by Frode and who team up with Peter after Frode leaves Waterford

Jarl-ship's captain. Trades frequently with Caen in Normandy

JORVIC (YORK)

Dag (cousin of Gustav, Freya's father) - Trader

Gudrun his wife

Hakon Their son and business partner

SAXON SETTLEMENT

Settlement chief   Cedric

His wife & Freya's business partner   Odella

NORMANDY (CAEN)

Halvar and Eira - Viking Danes-friends of Freya from England. Later, business partners in Frode's jewellery business, and his inheritors after Frode's death.

Hakon and Ingrid-friends of Jarl and hosts to Frode on arrival in Caen

Karl- trader

Olag-property owner

Harald-manufacturing jeweller and Frode's employer

Alfreirra and Margaret employees of Harald.

Frode and Freya's children – Gustav, Olaf, Iona.

William, Duke of Normandy, later known as "The Conqueror"

Petr and Andrew- shareholders in the Caen trading

 business.

Henri. Cavalry commander in Duke William's army. Friend and mentor of Gustav

Emma. Cousin of Duke William and wife of Gustaf (later Richard of Normandy, Count of Mortain).

Robert and Roald, their sons

CORNWALL (2013)

Tristan Penhaligan

Mary, his wife

Two children

MEASUREMENTS

Rode (Chapter Sixteen)
Accuracy is uncertain but is reckoned to be about 106 square feet. 25 Rode = approx. 2650sq.ft.

(Source reference: Viking Age Club & Society USA-Gary   Anderson)

THE VIKING AND THE LADY
THE STORY OF A PROPHECY COME TRUE

FOREWORD

A thousand years ago there were two friends (a boy and a girl) who grew up together and whose friendship, which became a deep love for each other, lasted several years. Later they had to spend a long time apart, but each never forgot the good times they shared. In accordance with a prophesy supported by the Viking Gods, they meet again in a land far away from their original home.

The story follows the fortunes of these children and their families originally living around Narvik in Nordland.

The environment is harsh and unforgiving, with months of semi darkness, bitter cold and violent storms. The monotony is relieved at times by brilliant light displays in the sky, watched with awe by the population. Farming and fishing are the main activities of the people, but these merely provide a subsistence level of life in a stunningly beautiful landscape of high mountain peaks covered with snow most of the year, and steep forested sides of fjords. However, the population is decreasing as more young men and some young women move on to seek their fortunes elsewhere.

Fewer return than leave. History has been unkind to the Vikings. It is true they sacked and pillaged where pickings were easy (such as Lindisfarne Abbey), and moved against local populations but they did settle in the areas of their incursions soon afterwards. Marriage with local people was common. King Harold Bluetooth commanded the Viking Danes to become Christian, albeit to protect his people from invasion by the Holy Roman Empire, leading to a rapid conversion of Vikings elsewhere. The result was Vikings becoming far less warlike as they were absorbed into the populations of the lands they settled in.

The Vikings were essentially explorers and traders with great sailing and trading skills. They were tough and resourceful, essential to survival in Nordland. They travelled to the Orkney and Shetland Islands, North East Scotland and established colonies in Dublin (Dyflin) in 841 and York (Jorvic) in around 866. They also settled in Iceland, Greenland and they reached North America around the year 1000. They founded the biggest settlement outside Iceland in Normandy and intermarried with the local population eventually to become known as "The Normans."

They even reached the Middle East on trading via the river network in Europe. They formed part of the bodyguard of the Sultan of Constantinople.

In this story "The Viking" is called Frode (meaning "enlightened and wise") after the Viking God; he is a skilled storyteller, learning from his grandfather; he is a wanderer by nature. His family are farmers, he being the youngest of four children born to Eric and Gyda (one boy and three girls).

"The Lady" is called Freya, after the Goddess of fertility and love. She is the second of three children of Gustav and Ranveya (one boy and two girls) and is fiercely protected by her older brother Harid.

Frode and Freya are about the same age and, as children, play with friends where, in winter especially, Frode often entertains them with stories, told in the established tradition, and ones which he makes up. Even adults are enthralled by his humour and inventiveness.

He works with Freya to produce short plays, acted by their childhood friends, bringing to life Frode's stories.

The story unfolds as the two are separated for some years, (in the story, "The Separation Years").

They never forget each other, and then they come together in Normandy, after periods of living and working in England and Ireland. They marry and establish a commercial dynasty, in fulfilment of a prophesy.

The story continues, exploring the early development of the dynasty in Cornwall, England, after the Norman Conquest.

The story comes full circle in a vision to Tristan Penhaligon, a descendant of Frode and Freya, in Normandy in 2013. In the vision Tristan is charged with researching the dynastic history of the family and with writing a book as a permanent record. He is also charged with producing a verbal version from 2017 onwards at the annual Festival of Cornish Literature and Folklore held at the Indian Queen's Pit in Fraddon, Cornwall.

Tristan and his wife Mary work together for three years travelling to Norway, York (Jorvic), Dublin (Dyflyn), Wexford (Ireland), Normandy and spending long periods in Cornwall.

On completion of their travels they work to analyse the results of their research. Tristan feels that he does not have to write a chronicle, nor does he want to. He and Mary decide that the story should end sometime after the Norman invasion of England, when the dynasty is established.

Tristan decides that he should test the reaction to his story by taking the piece about the plays Frode and Freya produced in Nordland when they were children, presenting them to audiences in Fowey.

He finds that children are interested, but more and more adults are drawn to him. He goes further, showing Frode's brooch to his audiences, carefully explaining its origins and significance.

Some audiences show interest in other Viking stories and he finds himself producing more stories while avoiding blood- thirsty tales and concentrating on the trading and sailing skills. He has a friend make a large model of a longboat which holds the children's interest.

As the tourist season progresses he is certain that he has got it right and makes his final preparations for his presentation at the Fraddon Festival.

Tristan's story follows…

PROLOGUE

CAEN NORMANDY FRANCE- SUMMER 2013

FOWEY CORNWALL AUTUMN 2016
FRADDON CORNWALL SUMMER 2017

It is a glorious summer day in Caen. Tristan Penhaligon, his wife, Mary, and their 2 young children are on holiday in Normandy from Bodmin in Cornwall. The family owns the biggest fishing organisation in Cornwall, established over centuries and has relations in Normandy. Tristan has retired as chairman of the company and is renowned as a storyteller. He spends time entertaining his children and their friends at birthday parties and family gatherings. He is often entreated by children to "tell us a story, tell us a story!" He is a leading light in a story telling group in Fowey; particularly at the annual festival designed to keep Cornish folklore alive at the Fraddon Festival. He frequently intersperses his tales with ones he has made up, or stories from other cultures. He is puzzled by his finding himself wanting to tell stories of Vikings.

He entertains tourists visiting the beautiful harbour at Fowey with his stories, during the tourist season. Tristan, tall and slim with blond hair, has piercing green eyes. He has travelled widely, and from his experiences, has built up a fund of stories. His main hobby is to preserve Cornish folklore. He sticks strictly to the truth where it can be verified, and to speculate where it cannot; he is not above embellishing his tales- particularly for children.

The family has decided to visit a park in central Caen, when on holiday in Normandy, well renowned for its magnificent mini lakes and the variety of its wild fowl. Mary takes the children off to see the wild fowl while Tristan relaxes in the sun.

He has a strange feeling as the atmosphere darkens and chills slightly. He looks up and sees a vision before him, shimmering in the subdued light. It is of a tall beautiful woman with her head held high from which falls hair in long tresses, dressed in the Viking style of a woman of substance, wearing a full length dark green cloak with a cream coloured shawl. He notices an exquisitely made brooch made of silver showing runic signs and with amber pieces set into it. He is amazed to see it is identical to one Mary wears from time to time. It has been in the family for as along as anyone can remember and he knows that it has always been handed down through the male line of the family and worn by their wives. No-one knows of its origins but is believed to have protection powers for its owner. Here is a mystery solved and he decides to tell Mary.

The vision speaks, "I am Freya, your ancestor, and I was reunited after many years of separation, with my true love, and later husband, Frode, in this very place over 1000 years ago. He was a revered storyteller. We founded a dynasty, which has lasted for centuries. Over those centuries I have been waiting for a descendant matching his skill to research the family history. You are that person and I want you to present a great love story verbally in the traditional Viking way at a Folk Festival in Cornwall. I want to ensure the family's Viking ancestry is never forgotten. I also want to remind you and Mary of the purpose and power of the brooch she is wearing as I know these have been forgotten."

Freya pauses, then reaches out to him. He takes her hand in his and for a few moments he feels drawn into her mind, realising in the process that he is being entrusted with a wonderful mission. She gently squeezes his hand, smiles a dazzling smile,"sadly, I am not allowed by the Gods to appear to you again, but I shall continue to watch over you and your family."

With that she is gone; The light grows stronger and the chill disappears. A little while later Mary returns with the children who are noisily arguing about which was the prettiest duck. Mary stops and looks at Tristan,"you look strange, are you feeling O.K?"

Tristan, with a dreamy look in his eyes, replies, "I have just had the most enchanting experience."

Mary, with gentle chuckling, "I suppose you have had an inspiration for a new story!"

Tristan laughs, "well yes-let me explain. I can tell you too of the origin of the brooch!"

He tells Mary of the vision and of the task he has been set.

On returning to Bodmin they agree that Tristan should investigate local folklore stories, visiting museums and libraries. Extensive reading will be necessary, covering old manuscripts and books.

Over that time Tristan visits Narvik and Oslo in Norway, the Shetland Islands, and Fraserburgh in Scotland. He spends months in Dublin and York where the Vikings had established very large settlements. He also visits the monastery at Glendalough and Waterford in Ireland. He returns to Caen several times.

His research is also spent increasing his knowledge of the family history in Cornwall, knowing that his family has deep roots there.

Tristan and Mary settle down to assemble and study all the material they have gathered; then Tristan begins to build the story.......

CHAPTER ONE

A VIKING SETTLEMENT IN NORDLAND AROUND NARVIK IN SPRING 1002

The story begins in Narvik, a Viking settlement of around 100 people located some 130 miles north of what is to become known in later times as the Arctic Circle and about 1600 miles south of the North Pole. The climate is harsh and unforgiving; daylight hours are very short in winter.

The Vikings are mainly farmers and fishermen. They are also a seafaring people well known as traders, explorers, and warriors. Those who suffer Viking raids do not recognise that Vikings also come to establish trade and settle. They also seek opportunities to enlist as mercenaries where they can. Christian monasteries are poorly defended, and plundering is irresistible.

Because of the harsh weather in their homeland, coupled with poor farming conditions, many Vikings seek survival elsewhere. Perversely, perhaps, many Vikings return to their homes each year, bringing with them plunder, slaves, and goods to enable them to survive yet another winter. Narvik's population lives in 5 longhouses and other smaller hut-type buildings, built of timber with thatched roofs. Each longhouse holds up to 3 families along with provision for shelter for their livestock. There is also a building used for meetings by the community's ruling body-The Elders. The buildings are arranged in a way that creates a central area for recreational, social, and other communal activities.

All is quiet in the settlement, but Frode, aged 8, is tossing and turning in his bed as are most of the children in the settlement. For tomorrow is the day when the people gather together to celebrate the continued prosperity of the settlement and to give thanks to the Nordic Gods for their bounty. The festivities include a feast, the giving of presents to the children and the telling of a Saga, the topic being selected by the Elders, with the storyteller, a member of the community. Frode is to be this year's storyteller and he is very nervous.

He is to present his story in the centre of the settlement. His selection is unprecedented as the role always goes to an adult. However, Frode's reputation as a storyteller has led the Elders to try an experiment.

"Why not give this very talented boy an opportunity to show his talent to all?" the Elders suggest.

Because he is so young his grandfather is allowed to be close to him so that he is not overwhelmed.

The basic story he tells is a traditional one. The storyteller is expected to introduce subtle changes and emphases which are then discussed by the Elders who decide which changes are worthy of being added to the story for the future.

Frode has been taught by his grandfather. Though he still has much to learn, he is thrilled and honoured to have been selected. He has chosen to tell a story that relates to the foundation of a settlement on an island out to the west beyond the horizon. At the end he will introduce a feature never used before. He will make a prophesy.

Frode has no idea where the inspiration has come from, nor of the source of the courage to depart so radically from tradition.

At mid-morning the weather is calm with a light frost covering the grass. Against a backdrop of snow-capped high mountain peaks, all the people of the settlement gather round the central area in which a low rostrum has been built.

The senior Elder, dressed in full ceremonial garb, mounts the rostrum, holds his hands high and waits for the spectators to settle down. He then announces, "today we celebrate the continued success of our settlement and we give thanks to our Gods for their protection and bounty".

He continues." As you know we offer the Gods a story in thanks. For this year we decided to depart from tradition by selecting young Frode, who has entertained us for some time with his stories."

The Elder calls Frode to the rostrum, takes him by the hand, holds his arm aloft, and calls, "Pray the Gods favour Frode and hear him well!"

The spectators roar their approval.

Frode takes a deep breath, sweeps his eyes over the crowd which becomes hushed in anticipation.

He announces in a strong voice, belying his nerves,

"My people, I am deeply honoured to have been chosen to present the traditional annual story. I offer you my thanks." He pauses, then continues,

"I will develop an established theme, that of the foundation of a settlement on a small island out to the west beyond the horizon, which is fertile, green and prosperous. As you know that settlement was created by our forebears many, many years ago. I will also introduce something new which I will reveal to you later."

Frode has the audience spellbound as he brings the story to life in a way that has never been heard before, crafting his words to create colourful living pictures in their minds. He re-creates the story of the trials, tribulations, and triumphs of the people in a settlement named Dyflin on this wonderful island. Dyflin is not the only settlement created by Viking adventurers, but Frode concentrates on Dyflin. Having done so he declaims, "now I come to the feature I promised to tell you about. I offer a prophesy for your approval and that of our Gods."

He pauses while an air of expectation in the audience is palpable. Then he speaks," I prophesy that two people of this settlement will come together after a long separation in a land far to the south and who will forge a dynasty that achieves great power and influence lasting far into the future. I cannot reveal who these two people are. I have not been entrusted with that information. In due time all will be revealed, and they will know who they are."

He then moves to the front of the rostrum, kneels, and prays,

"Gods of our race, accept this tribute made on behalf of all our people and grant support and ultimate success in the fulfilment of the prophesy."

He then stands and bows to the audience.

There is a silence for a few moments and then waves of applause break out. His grandfather moves to his side, takes him in his arms,

"you've done it lad-I am proud of you."

What Frode cannot, and must not know yet, is that his grandfather realises that Frode has spoken of his own destiny.

In the crowd there is a girl of about the same age, called Freya, who, becoming conscious of something she cannot explain, goes very quiet. Her mother notices, as Freya is not renowned for being quiet, and asks, "are you alright?"

Freya nods and replies hesitantly, "yes mother."

Her mother has a premonition that she is observing something quite profound, as Freya remains thoughtful. She resolves to remain quietly watchful.

Meantime, confusion reigns because the people do not know how to deal with a prophesy. However, the Elders, calling for patience, go to the meeting house to consider what to do. They have been surprised by Frode's audacity. It does not take them long to conclude that this development is inspired by the Gods and, therefore, must be encouraged and that they should advise their people to support the prophesy, invoking, as Frode did, the blessings of the Gods.

After a short while the Elders return and the senior Elder steps up to the front of the rostrum addressing the crowd, "we have agreed Frode's prophesy is inspired by the Gods and have, therefore, agreed that the prophesy should enter our folklore, to be told as a separate story at the annual gathering. In this way we can ensure that the prophesy is held safe in our minds until it is fulfilled."

The people acclaim the decision with cheers and clapping hands while Frode is surrounded by well- wishers.

Meantime, little Freya is quietly pondering.

The children shriek delightedly while the presents are distributed, and they scamper away to play with them.

Meantime all is subsumed in the feasting and jollity of the occasion.

Freya moves quietly to Frode's side and suggests they both move away from the crowd. They sit down and Freya, looking at Frode asks, "Why did you make the prophesy?"

Frode, turns his gaze from the crowd of revellers, "Freya, I just do not know, it just came to me. Maybe it has been inspired by the Gods"

Freya then has a flash of inspiration. She jumps up, her face alight with pleasure and exclaims, "wouldn't it be fun if we were the couple to forge the dynasty?"

Frode, missing the point, not being enamoured of the idea, does not answer, and remains deep in thought.

Freya, piqued by Frode's lack of perception, turns away and rushes off to join the festivities, while wiping away tears.

Frode continues to sit alone, his mind in a turmoil. He is not to know that he is not yet mature enough to read the signals offered by Freya. He eventually wanders off to join the party, having not the slightest idea of the train of events he has set in motion.

Unbeknown to each they are being watched by Harid…

CHAPTER TWO

THE VIKING SETTLEMENT IN NORDLAND AROUND NARVIK 1002 TO 1010.

FRODE

Following Frode's triumph at the story-telling event, his life returns to that of a child in the settlement.

He is the youngest of four children. While nearly all his friends are absorbed by tales of fighting and exploration, Frode is gentle of nature and is interested in exploring the background to the Sagas and the use of language to express ideas and descriptions of events; he is a dreamer. The farm is a prosperous one, having 30 head of cattle, a flock of 60 sheep, goats, and several dogs. Cereals and vegetables are grown. The family is regarded as wealthy and they occupy a longhouse with two other families.

Frode's main task in the family is to tend the sheep, while his siblings share all the other farming and domestic tasks to help their parents. He has ample opportunity to sit and dream, think up stories. Frode's father is close to his grandfather (who has devoted many hours telling Frode stories) and both agree that his destiny has been planned by the Gods and lies beyond the farm in Narvik. Frode always seeks the company of returning sailors and fishermen so that they can regale him with tales of great adventures.

Frode, now 10 years old, is well built, with unruly blond hair which is often long enough to hide his bright green eyes. So much so, that to the amusement of his friends, he cannot always see where he is going. He has an ill-disciplined sense of humour that helps him master the ups and downs of his life; more often it gets him into trouble, especially with the girls. One of them, Freya, is intrigued by him, admiring his sharp, agile mind. She is always caught up in his stories and often feels an affinity with one character who appears quite frequently in his tales of the sea.

She is very much in love with him and uses her feminine wiles (well developed in one so young) to attract him. She is constantly finding reasons to be at his side. She dresses with style, learning from her mother. She is frustrated as Frode is completely unaware of her feelings.

He, and his friends spend lots of time exploring the shore of the fiord nearby, fishing, trekking into the hinterland and visiting the longship building yards further up the fiord. In between they play knatteikr, involving striking a ball with a bat, where the striker is chased by the opposition while running to a point some distance away.

Tackling is fearsome, but if the runner reaches the end target a point is scored. The girls are a true match for the boys, giving no quarter in the tackle. The game is popular with the children playing it most days. Games of wrestling and skating are popular in winter.

As the boys become older they indulge in oar jumping, involving running along the oars of a longship without falling off. Not so easy as the crew roll the oars over. It is a dangerous sport as falling into the freezing fjord waters can be fatal if the contestant is not rescued quickly enough.

The scenery is breath-taking; it is little wonder that a child of Frode's sensitivity is captivated by it all. Frode is very skilful at mixing his work with the family sheep and his leisure activities.

One day, just after his eleventh birthday, Frode and his friends Gustav, Hortha, Lodi, Inga, Margaretha, and Freya are down on the shore of the fiord. It is Spring; the sun is shining in a cloudless sky; the wind is light for once and the sea quite calm. Frode is deeply engaged in searching for crabs in a rock pool. He looks up and is thrilled to see several fully laden merchant longships passing by, the water running off the oars flashing in the sunlight. They are accompanied by three warships for protection. The sail on each is being raised to the accompaniment of the crews chanting.

He shouts to the others, "Look, the longships are going out!"

All stop what they are doing and leap about waving their arms yelling, "Sail well and come back safely."

The warship crews respond by banging the shields lining the hulls with their swords. For Frode it is a turning point in his life. He resolves,

"I must go on a longship to explore the world. I want to collect stories and tell them whenever and wherever I can."

He explains his ambition to his friends as they sit on the rocks chatting. Frode does not notice the light of hero worship in Freya's eyes as she now clearly understands what has been in her mind since the day of Frode's story presentation. She turns to her best friend, Margaretha, saying, "I love this boy; I feel my life is bound to his."

Margaretha, with all the "wisdom" of a 10-year-old, comments, "Ugh-he's such an arrogant little brute. He's all yours!"

Freya realises that she has competition and resolves to watch Margaretha very carefully indeed.

FREYA

Freya is the second of three children, in a farming family having their farm adjacent to Frode's. Their farm is larger than Frode's; the family is the richest in the settlement, and occupy a longhouse of their own, albeit smaller than a shared longhouse. She is tall for her age, has long hair and dresses with an elegance way beyond her years. By tradition, however, she, as a child, is not allowed to wear jewellery, except brooches used to hold material together. She takes advantage of this and has brooches of intricate designs made, thanks to a friendship with the jewellery maker of the settlement. She spends much time with him and learns many of the skills and secrets of the trade.

Her green eyes are constantly watchful; they do not miss much. Her intelligence makes her a leading member of a group of seven children who are together as often as family duties allow.

Freya is developing skills in weaving woollen garments, using imaginative patterns, for herself and the family. Her grandmother spends time teaching her to use the weaving frames her father has built for her.

Her main problem is that her older brother, Harid, has appointed himself her protector and she is constantly at loggerheads with him over his interfering and intrusive behaviour. He is not part of the crowd as he is a bully, quite unpleasant, and he is forever lurking on the fringes of the friends' activities, watching. He has been doing this since the day of Frode's story. Freya, as is required in Viking society, aids her mother in cooking, weaving, spinning, and managing the domestic scene. She is close to her grandmother who talks of the family history in a society where traditions are handed down orally. In her family, the tradition is for the grandmother to ensure the preservation of the histories. Freya has, until recently, shown no real interest, just patiently listening as is her duty.

Today is the day that Frode sees the longboats going down the fiord and he draws his friends into listening to a story he wants to tell about the great expeditions their forebears have undertaken in the longboats. He weaves a tale of adventure, dangers overcome, and the wonders in other lands beyond the sea, speaking for an hour or more.

Freya, listening, like the others, is enthralled by the magic of Frode's story telling. She has noticed that a woman features in all his sea tales and she is intrigued. In a pause in the story she asks Frode, "who is the lady?"

"She is a Viking Goddess, Sjofn, Goddess of harmony and human love."

Privately Frode sees Freya as The Lady. He then sees a chance to devise an entirely new angle to his tale. Frode then proceeds to tell them, (making it up as he goes along), "this is the Goddess who, being a minor God in the Viking pantheon of Gods, is nonetheless very important, caring for the welfare of seafarers and explorers."

Freya being in a romantic and playful mood, jumps up and shouts, "let's play explorers. I want to be Sjofn!"

Frode, not liking losing control of his audience, rebukes her, "you must let me finish my story. Then we can talk about acting out the story."

However, he cannot resist teasing her, and with a wicked grin he says, "if you are good I might let you play the part of Sjofn, but only when, and if, I decide that we make the stories into plays."

Freya is furious and pulls a face at him. In his teasing of her he begins to realise that he cares for her very much.

Frode's story is of the crew of a longboat far from land. It is lost, caught in a furious storm. Sjofn appears to the crew, calms them with gentle words of love and caring. She helps the captain regain his sense of direction. The storm abates through Sjofn's intercession with Thor, the senior Norse God. The longboat safely reaches Hjaltland.

The play takes many weeks to plan, to guide the children through how to invent dialogue, and how to act. Freya's natural acting talent, together with her organising skills, help her do this. The children have no costumes or props and it is to their imagination that Freya looks. Frode sees the problem Freya has. There is no effective means of writing down the dialogue as Viking culture is largely an oral one. When it does come to recording things, writing things down is of limited application. The Runic script is difficult to learn, and it is rare for a 10-year-old to have the experience and skill to use it properly. The recording media, waxed tablets, wood sticks and stone, are not conducive to Frode's purpose.

He suggests a solution to Freya, "why not consider my telling the story at the side of the stage, with the children, under your direction, acting the parts as I describe them?" He continues," the children can invent the dialogue to match the scene and interpret all the actions under your direction."

Freya realises immediately that this is the solution, "Frode, that's brilliant! Let's try it."

They try out the idea and agree that this is actually the way to do it. Then they all practice and practice until a production is fit to be presented to an audience. Frode and Freya are astounded and pleased by the enthusiasm and skills shown by the children.

When the scenes are finished and the whole play is ready to be presented, he draws Freya to one side, "why don't we work together, with my telling the story, as we have just done, with you organising the plays?"

Frode is excited by this and thinks that maybe the stories should become short plays to be presented to the people from the settlement, even on the big story telling day.

He holds Freya's hands, saying, "let's do short plays to entertain our people-particularly during the long winter evenings. I'd love to work with you!"

Freya immediately sees the pleasure she will gain from this closeness to Frode. Inclining her head coquettishly, she smiles winsomely and agrees, "that would be lovely. Let's do it."

Ever impulsive she cries, "Let's go talk to the Elders right now. We could always present this play to them as a way of convincing them."

Freya thinks out loud, "there is a problem-as there is no building big enough to house the audience. In addition, we'd need help from the adults in making costumes and props. We'd also need the Elders' help in persuading the adults that we have something worthwhile to do. The adults are forever moaning that us young people do nothing but loaf about."

Both have meetings with the Elders and some other adults, who quickly support the idea and consider the question of how to solve the problem of providing a building to house the performances. Open air performances are usually out of the question because of the weather. Then the idea of creating a very large tent would be feasible, provided it was heavily tied down to protect it from damage by fierce winds. Each performance could be spread over a period of days so as to present to as many people as possible. The tent can be erected and dismantled quite easily. Frode fails to see, but Freya does, the look of horror on their friend Margaretha's face as she watches the friendship grow stronger. Frode is blissfully unaware of the trouble that may lie ahead. To complicate matters, Freya's brother, Harid, is lurking on the fringes of the group as always. He resolves that he must ensure that the intimacy he just seen is stopped.

The next five years are idyllic for Frode, Freya, and the children as they work together growing to maturity. They put on two short plays a year with enormous success. More than once the tent is destroyed by storms, but the people work together to replace it. The Elders agree to the inclusion of short plays in the annual story telling event as an integral part of the occasion.

While Freya is deeply in love with Frode during the years of collaboration. On those occasions that she tries to show her love, he is unresponsive. He, in fact, is very shy and is not comfortable with the feelings he has towards Freya. Freya's problem is that she does not want to spoil the relationships within the group, and withdraws within herself, hoping that one day Frode will acknowledge her.

Freya is committed to working with Frode as their confidence as story tellers and players grows. They are feted by audiences every time they put forward a production of stories of children's adventures sailing the fiords and adventures when exploring. The children are very talented and are a joy to work with.

Harid believes that Margaretha can easily divert Frode's attention from his sister. Margaretha realises that Frode's is totally committed to producing the stories and plays and not too keen on romance. Surprisingly, Harid's attitude softens as he gets older and the children feel he need not be excluded. He is accepted into the group and is secretly thrilled to be among the others sharing in the fellowship and the fun. Harid, has a fine singing voice, so songs are built into the stories, much to the delight of everybody, not least Harid. Nonetheless, he keeps a careful eye on Freya.

THE CHILDREN GROW UP

At 15-years-of-age, Freya is coming to know matters of love as she grows to womanhood, its many delights, and problems. She is relying on intuition, observation and help from her mother and grandmother. Her mother is watching her closely and sees Freya's love for Frode. Wisely, she keeps her counsel for the moment. Freya, having attained womanhood, is free to express herself through her clothing. She has been longing to do this for a long time. She has been learning about spinning and weaving from her mother and grandmother, showing a flair for design and style. She loves experimenting and for everyday use, while maintaining design style, producing several woollen dresses and overdresses, using brooches she has designed with the guidance of her friend, the jeweller, to hold the elements together. The natural dyes available to her are many and varied, giving her the chance to experiment with mixtures of assorted colours. The brooches compliment the colours and shades she uses when coupled with braids having intricate motifs. She has tried to incorporate pictures of animals and other aspects of life within her designs. While this indicates her use of her fertile imagination, the work is technically beyond her for the moment. She vows to her mother, "I will keep trying."

In the meantime, Frode constantly remembers his vow to himself about travelling away from Narvik. He is nearing 16 years old: he is restless and ready to test his mettle in the outside world. He is now six feet tall, fair haired, strongly built and despite his interest in cultural things, is no weakling. He has cultivated a thick beard which Freya secretly detests. He is still inclined to be a dreamer. His friends are in the same state of suppressed excitement as changes are imminent. It does not look as though a play will be produced this year. Even the Elders think that the youngsters have outgrown the activity.

His grandfather has become very frail and Frode consults with him more often. One day his mother sends one of his sisters to the field where he is tending the sheep to tell him,"come quickly, Grandpa is unwell.

Frode rushes to his grandfather's bedside to find the old man having difficulty in breathing. Grandfather beckons to Frode to come close.

Slowly he whispers to Frode, "the Gods say that you and Freya are bound together, but you are not destined to be close for years to come. Remember the prophesy you made? She will be your lady in a place far from here. In the meantime, follow your destiny as a wandering storyteller and bring happiness to those whom you meet."

With that grandfather, being a former Viking warrior, leaves on his journey to Valhalla.

Frode weeps and wanders off, in a distraught state of mind, up the shore of the fiord to build a shelter from materials he finds nearby.

Frode stays by the fiord, in the shelter he has built, for many days, grieving. His sisters visit him with food and water trying to console him. Freya comes to see him on the advice of his sisters, but being fearful of intruding, just sits next to him. Eventually they start talking and Frode at last fully realises that his Grandfather was right. This lovely caring girl is a joy to be with. Freya must return home before dark as she cannot stay, however much she wants too. Each day she returns to Frode and by talking and enjoying each other's company Frode becomes himself again.

Surely, he thinks, "this girl and I are meant to be together always."

There is a problem in that he cannot suppress the desire to go on his journey, and seek his fortune, as many young men before him have done. A little later he asks Freya to walk with him to the side of the fiord. He explains, as they walk, "It is my destiny to go on a long journey. I have come to love you and as I think you feel the same way. I believe we are the couple in the prophesy."

Freya, overcome with joy, puts her arms around his neck and they kiss passionately.

They swear fealty to each other and express the hope that they really are the couple of the prophesy.

Soon an expedition is being assembled and he, along with some of his friends, asks to join it. They all are given their parents' consent and support. Freya gives her blessing.

Frode and his friends go to the port along the fiord to meet the longship captains, and where they are accepted for training which they know will be rigorous.

There are a few girls from the settlement who are attracted to the idea of adventure and fighting. Freya is not one of them as Harid has persuaded their parents to insist that she must remain with the family to do her duty. Freya is unhappy, but she knows that she must defer to her parent's demand. The boys are nervous about girls joining, but the experienced sailors welcome them, if only as a diversion. Early on, however, the girls show that they are not to be under-estimated and before the expedition sets out, matters have settled down. The girl have earned the respect of the travel-hardened sailors during training.

Frode takes his duties seriously. He has to as there are no concessions to perceived weakness. Before the expedition sets out there is a huge farewell party with singing, dancing, and heavy drinking. Freya views the festivities with great sadness, seeing the end of a wonderful part of her life. Harid is watching her, even though he knows Freya is not joining the expedition. Freya sees an opportunity to move away from Harid and get close to Frode. She whispers in his ear, " I love you to distraction. I know that we will meet again but, in the meantime, please, please take care of yourself."

She must move away and then realises that Frode probably has not heard her due to the noise of the celebrations. She knows Frode loves her too and, as she turns away, Frode reaches out and gives her a warm embrace.

Harid sees this but is unable to do anything about it. By now he is not even sure he wants to, as he realises he is in danger of losing his sister's love. Freya, deeply upset, leaves the party to find a quiet place at the edge of the settlement to think. She realises that weeping, whilst natural, prevents clarity of thought.

As she vows not to spend her life with anyone else other than Frode, she knows now that all is not lost, so long as she believes the prophesy relates to her and Frode. She draws comfort from this and resolves to get on with her life in the settlement.

On returning to her house she finds her mother waiting, who takes her in her arms and comforts her. "Have patience," she advises. All will come to pass in time."

Freya then realises that her mother believes, or knows, that she and Frode are the subject of the prophesy.

As Freya calms down Ranveya confirms this by saying, "we believe you and Frode have been chosen by the Gods. However, they will want to be sure that you will both be worthy of the task they are entrusting you with."

"What do you mean?" sniffles Freya.

"We are sure the Gods have devised a plan that involves both of you facing challenges. Your finding solutions to these challenges will prepare you to have and to bring up children in a loving caring home that will give them the skills and determination to create the dynasty."

Freya is mollified by Ranveya's council and decides to go to bed. In the morning Freya goes to Ranveya and, giving her a warm hug, whispers in her ear, "thanks for your wisdom and advice last night."

"I advised as a loving mother should. In the future you will do the same for your children. It is a mother's role in life."

Freya replies, "I need time to think so I am going for a long walk.

"Sounds a good idea,"

Freya calls on Margaretha and asks her," would you walk with me; I need your advice."

Margaretha, is non plussed, "of course. I hope I can help."

Freya then reminds Margaretha of the prophesy made by Frode, the meaning she feels is behind it and how, despite all the indications, particularly from her mother, she just cannot accept the possibility of her being part of the prophesy.

Margaretha listens with increasing wonder as Freya tells the story. At the end Margaretha is quite sure what Freya must do. "Freya, follow your destiny no matter what happens."

Freya hugs Margaretha. "Thank you for understanding, I shall take your advice. Can you stay close to me over the next few years as I think I shall be facing a long lonely time wondering if Frode is safe and well?"

Margaretha, thrilled to be trusted says, " of course, I'd be proud to be your friend and confident."

CHAPTER THREE

THE SEPARATION YEARS

FRODE LEAVES NARVIK

Before the expedition sets out, all of the people from the surrounding settlements gather together at the shore and chant the Viking Prayer-

"May the Gods of Asgard guide your steps towards their gates.

In your journey, may it be safe and filled with light. May you find strength from Thor in your darkest hours. May you find wisdom from Odin in times of confusion.

May you find beauty and lasting bonds from Freya and Frey.

May your web be spun tightly with that which makes you stronger, happy and wise.

And may the gods always look upon you with good grace."

The expedition, comprising three longships protected by two warships, sets off on a pleasant summer morning on a trading mission to Dyflin. Everyone on board is in high spirits. Frode, however, is overcome by a melancholy and admits to himself, "I am missing Freya so much already."

Soon, however, he puts his thoughts aside so that he can attend to his duties; the captain does not tolerate any slackness. The longships leave the mouth of the fiord and enter the open sea.

Frode, once he recovers from his melancholy, is feeling excited about what lies ahead. He is a little fearful as he has been told so many stories of the perils of sea voyages. Now he knows he is about to find out for himself at first hand. The first port of call is Hjaltland where they are to deliver and collect goods, land some settlers, take on supplies and make repairs. As the sea is moderate it is expected that repairs will be minimal. However, the sea Gods have a habit of launching sudden and violent storms to catch the unwary and everybody on board must take their turn at keeping a weather lookout.

Prayers to the Goddess Sjofn are made morning and evening in supplication for a safe journey. Sjofn is always watching out for any sneaky tricks by the sea Gods and being ready to counter them. She is not always successful in the face of very powerful Gods such as Aegir and his partner Ran who love giving parties for other gods and then playing practical jokes on unwary sailors. Sjofn is a very busy Goddess.

The boats arrive safely in Hjaltland. While passengers and cargo are being dealt with Frode takes advantage of shore leave and goes to visit a local family. In a society which craves news Frode is made welcome.

Bjorn, head of the household, asks, "do tell us all the news from Narvik."

Frode is immediately in his element,

"After our meal let us all sit round the fire and I will tell you all that has been going on in Narvik"

Bjorn goes out to invite the neighbours in.

After the meal is over Frode immediately captivates his audience, "I will first give you the news and then I will tell you an exciting story of children in Narvik who formed a group to present plays based upon stories I created."

Frode proceeds to entertain the family and friends for the rest of the evening.

At the end Bjorn asks,"would you like to tell these stories to other families here?"

"While I must go on to Dyflin in a few days I would be happy to do as you ask."

Bjorn organises for Frode to move about the family groups presenting his stories. As he does so he collects more stories to add to his repertoire. While he is touring around he has attracted the attention of a shy and very attractive girl called Fiona. This is not really surprising as Frode is an extremely charismatic young man, but he has no desire to be disloyal to Freya. He is focused on his intention to explore the world and, since Fiona is shy and unable to express her interest openly, nothing develops between them.

After five days the longboat captains call in their crews, restock the provisions and take some passengers for Dyflin on board. They set sail and proceed over the north of Scotland, knowing that this is the most dangerous part of the voyage. The area is known for its violent storms and rough seas. Sure enough they encounter a storm and it takes the crew's skill, with prayers to the Goddess Sjofn, to keep control of the ship. Frode and the crew work hard to take down the sail. The captain is constantly shouting above the roar of the wind, "row, row, row" while he and two crew members man the steering oar, which requires all their strength to maintain their course.

After several hours the storm abates, and the crew can hoist the sail again. The captain of Frode's longboat calls, "let us give thanks to Sjofn for our deliverance and ask her to give us smooth passage to Dyflin"

Frode mutters to a sailor next to him, "I don't know how you cope with this. Give me dry land every time!"

His companion snorts in derision, "weakling!"

Frode is minded to retaliate but the captain roars,"get on with it, there is no room for this nonsense. Sort it out later" Both men realise that they are being stupid and grin at each other as they get back to work.

All is not quite as smooth as they had hoped. The lookout cries,"ships approaching forward of us!"

The captain signals to the other longboats and the two escorting warships.

As four ships approach, it becomes clear to all that they are pirates. As the protecting warships turn to face the pirates, there is concern that two against four will not be enough to force the pirates to abandon their intent.

As battle ensues all the crews of the merchant longships can do is watch and wait. The captains of the escorting warships, with a display of seamanship and cunning, drive off the pirates accompanied by great cheers of the crews of the other ships.

There is concern that more pirates may join the defeated ones, so all the ships move closer together. Because the space between them is tight, the level of seamanship to avoid collisions is of the highest order. The seafaring skills learned by the Vikings over the centuries prove their worth.

Frode is amazed at the skills shown, for he has never considered the experience and skills needed to manage a longboat.

Days later they approach Dyflin through a magnificent bay with calm waters sparkling in the sun. Prayers to Sjofn have been answered and, once again, the crew gives thanks to her.

Frode now has the feeling that his great adventure has truly begun. He has also added the story of the voyage to his repertoire.

CHAPTER FOUR

THE SEPARATION YEARS

FREYA IN NARVIK

People of the settlement gather to watch the longships depart, Freya and those of the players who remain, stand quietly together in sadness. So many of these expeditions have led to fewer men returning than have set out. Freya, as she foreseeing the settlement dying, is overwhelmed by a sense of melancholy at seeing her lover sailing away.

She moves away from friends and returns to her house, crying gently, hoping no-one sees her. Ranveya does, but makes no move towards her, resolving to allow Freya her privacy overnight.

In the morning, Freya does not appear at normal time for breakfast. Her mother goes to her sleeping place, gently wakes her up and quietly says to her, "When you are ready we should talk. Meantime go get dressed and have some breakfast."

She leaves Freya who, reluctantly, has a brief wash, dresses, and goes to the eating area for breakfast. The other inhabitants of the longhouse sense Freya's grief and leave her in peace. After breakfast Ranveya nods to Freya indicating that they should retire to the quiet area

As Freya is being truculent, Ranveya speaks quietly to her, "Believe me, I know what you are feeling. I, too, had a similar experience."

She continues, while stroking Freya's hair soothingly, "tell me all about it as I have been aware of your feelings for Frode, probably before you even realised it. It's part of a mother's intuition. "Freya weeps and in a hesitant and shaky voice, says, "I hurt so much. I worship Frode for he is kind, gentle, clever, and funny. He is not brutal and talking of raids and conquest, like the other boys. I want to hear him telling his stories with my helping him produce the plays. I just want to be with him all the time."

"When I told him that I loved him at the farewell feast I had had only a few minutes out of Harid's sight. I told him I loved him again as I did before. He embraced me tightly which I have taken to mean that he was sincere when said he loved me too."

In a burst of weeping Freya is incoherent. Ranveya waits patiently until the storm passes and then decides that she should remind Freya of the meaning of the prophesy Frode made years ago. As Freya calms down, Ranveya says, "the prophesy Frode made and of which we are reminded each year is about you and Frode"

She continues, "You see, the two people in the prophesy who are going to create a dynasty in a land in the south are you and Frode. The Gods revealed this to the Elders before Frode spoke to the people"

Freya lowers her head. In a quiet voice tinged with more emotion she whispers, "I felt this was the meaning, but I just could not come to believe it. I am overwhelmed to know it is actually true rather than wishful thinking."

Ranveya takes Freya's hands in hers saying, "It is true; it has been determined by our Gods. As this settlement will eventually die because more people are leaving and not returning, you and Frode are to carry on our traditions into the future."

She stops, takes a breath, and continues, "however, it will be some years before you meet Frode again; the prophesy does not tell us when or where. In the meantime, you must play your part at home. I feel this may not be enough to stimulate your intellect and I think you should think about what you can do in addition to your household duties. It is important as the Gods indicated that you prepare yourself for the task they have mapped out for you. Only when the Gods believe you are ready will they allow you to meet again.

Freya is now completely convinced. She decides that she must apply all her energies to preparing herself to meet her destiny with pride and confidence.

Behind the scenes Goddess Freya indulges in a wistful smile happy that Freya has passed a major test.

CHAPTER FIVE

THE SEPARATION YEARS

FREYA IN BUSINESS

Over the ensuing weeks, whilst Freya misses Frode's company terribly, ideas come to mind, including one that she could design, make, and even sell women's clothes. She remembers the day, when they were all preparing costumes for a play, that Margaretha had made a remark on how dull clothes were and that she would like to do something about it. She seeks out Margaretha and explains her idea. Margaretha, enthusiastically claims, "this is wonderful. Count me in. Can I help plan how we are going to achieve it?"

"Oh, yes please!" Freya replies.

Freya goes to see her mother and father explaining, "I have an idea. I would like to design, make, and sell women's clothes. Margaretha is willing to be part of it. We are sure we have learned enough to do it and, father, you could train us to run a business and manage staff. What do you think?"

Gustav has a problem understanding the concept as there is no precedent for women running a business in Viking society in Nordland. He has heard that in big Viking settlements, business and the associated trading are well established, with women playing a significant part.

After much pondering he says, "there is no precedent for this up here, but there is no reason why you can't give it a try; you certainly have the determination to make it work, and there are numerous settlements in the area which should be big enough to provide regular custom. You will need to visit many of these settlements to see if people want to buy."

Freya and Margaretha invite Harid, Olaf and Runa from another family to join them in the enterprise. The five of them meet to discuss a business plan.

Harid identifies a problem and explains, "as we have no examples of our work without which we are missing a critical selling aid."

This puts a damper on matters until Harid explains, "we must invest the time and prepare samples of our work; then we have a real chance to make a success. You have shown you have the skills and I am sure you can persuade families to lend us their spinning and weaving frames when they are not being used, until we get our own."

Harid is proving to be an astute and deep-thinking young man. Everybody, admiring his enthusiasm, readily agree.

Olaf, a born trader, sets about doing deals to obtain small supplies of wool, and dyes, from local suppliers on a promise of regular custom when the business is set up. Freya, Margaretha, Harid and her father, Gustav, meet to establish the business.

Freya is determined to control the business and does this by getting agreement on who does what.

Gustav agrees to acquire the weaving and spinning frames. Freya, Margaretha and Runa will spin, weave, and make up the clothes, with help from other women. Freya will be the main designer as she has an idea that motifs and simple pictures can be incorporated into the weaves. She also understands the power of using colour. She has the thought that she could introduce "dream pictures" of Frode into some of her work.

Everybody works hard over the weeks preparing samples of weaving, colours, patterns, and designs for Harid and Olaf to use in their sales drive.

Harid and Olaf then go around the settlements explaining the business, showing the samples.

They will also offer to have customers' own designs incorporated in the weaves. If all goes well, when the business is ready, they will take orders for clothes.

The next need is for the acquisition of a large hut to work in. They will need space for spinning and weaving frames, dyeing vats, benches for finishing work and a store for raw materials such as wool and materials to provide dyes.

Gustav calls the team together and, in an atmosphere of great excitement, gives them a flying start.

"I will arrange and pay for the construction of the building in exchange for a share of the profits.

"How much?" queries Freya.

"Five per cent of your net profits for three years."

Freya is disposed to argue but then thinks better of it as she believes her father is being so generous and helpful.

"Agreed!"

She is aware that her parents are extremely wealthy, but she does not know that her father accumulated all this wealth from a short career raiding and pillaging in his youth.

She has learned an important aspect of being a successful businessperson. "Always play fair and give value for money while projecting an aura of honesty."

Freya is thrilled and while construction is under way the team gather materials together. Harid fixes agreements with local suppliers. Olaf has no problem arranging supplies of wool and dyes. Freya and Runa, work on the designs, patterns, and colours under Freya's direction.

She passionately believes that, apart from producing high quality garments, the imaginative use of colour, thereby banishing the dullness that has been bothering Margaretha, is the key to success. Surely, thinks Freya, "women must be attracted to bright fun colours!"

Freya did not expect such enthusiastic support from the older members of the community and, encouraged by this, starts to drive the business with the determination needed to be a success.

After many weeks of work a portfolio of designs is built up and sample weaves created. Margaretha is proving to have an extraordinary talent and compliments Freya's designs with some which are quite outlandish. Freya is more than happy to let her have a free hand.

Everybody works hard managing their assigned tasks. Freya holds regular discussions with them to monitor how things are going. Gustav sits in as financial adviser and contributes to solving problems that are constantly arising.

Harid is meeting resistance from potential customers who see no reason to move away from the tradition of families producing their own clothes. "It's time for us to unleash some of Margaretha's designs to create some shock," he thinks.

This proves very successful and Harid is able to present a substantial variety of designs. While Margarethe's wild designs appeal to young people to begin with, they have stimulated interest in Freya's use of colours.

Harid then has a radical idea, "why not invite potential customers to visit the workplace and see our colleagues in action?" he asks.

Many people take up the offer and are impressed by the processes being used which they know cannot easily be replicated in their own homes. Freya is asked if she would be prepared to sell the woven cloth, giving the buyer the opportunity to create their own garments. She readily agrees, and to exploit that part of the business, she has Gustav building another weaving frame, while she takes on another employee to produce the cloth.

By selling cloth she overcomes most people's resistance to her business.

Work gets started seriously with Freya and Margaretha spending one morning a week designing and the rest of the time spinning and weaving, making up clothes, and planning. Runa's main task now is weaving cloth for sale and orders for this are more frequent than for finished clothes.

Harid, having secured supplies of wool and dye making materials, is now able to visit the settlements selling cloth, showing design samples, and persuading ladies to order. Development is slow, not because of the lack of interest, rather a lack of money.

Freya considers using barter, but the business and the types of goods on offer makes this unsuitable. She feels that there is enough silver in circulation to support her business, but more modestly than she had hoped. Margaretha's wild and crazy colour mixes find favour with the

teenage girls who are clamouring for more and more dresses and shawls. She suggests to the team,"I think it would be worthwhile if I concentrated on this."

After some discussion the team agrees, and a spinning wheel and weaving frame are made for Margaretha's use.

Freya notices that Harid is often close to Margaretha and she begins to think that a romance is building. However, Margaretha seems too much absorbed in her work to be distracted, for the moment anyway.

The business enters a period of dedicated arduous work by everybody. Freya finds herself, at night before going to sleep, wondering how Frode is. She thinks, "is he safe and well? Would he be proud of me? Will I ever see him again as the prophesy foretells?"

She knows she is desperately in love with Frode; her only escape is to work, work, work. Her mother is observing this and is worried. She goes to Freya one evening after their meal, saying, "you must slow down. Listen to Margaretha and watch how she takes breaks to relieve the pressure. Become ill and your business will be at risk of failing. Remember that the prophesy-it will come true. Our Gods do not lie!"

Freya promises to take her mother's advice, however hard it will be.

After several months of canvassing for business with little success and, as Freya is getting depressed, a wonderful thing happens. Harid has taken Margaretha with him to Harstad, some twenty miles away up the coast, because he believes her vivacious nature will win over the young people to wanting cloth worked to her magical designs. He also has an ulterior motive, he wants Margaretha alone with him.

Ten days after setting out they return full of enthusiasm and with orders for many bales of cloth.

To Freya this is the breakthrough she has been praying for. She calls the team together with other members of the families and addresses them, "Harid and Margaretha have returned with orders for 20 bales of cloth. Let us congratulate them." Everybody gives a rousing cheer. "Now," claims Freya, "let's get down to work and show our customers what we can do."

Freya and Harid get down to planning the production runs. Freya draws Margaretha to aside and comments, "You two are in love, aren't you?"

Margaretha, blushing, "yes, but we want to devote our energies to helping you build your business. Then we shall see"

Freya is reassured and gives Margaretha a big hug. Harid, who comes upon the scene, is unsure what to do until his sister turns on him and gives him a hug as well.

The business concentrates on producing cloth rather than finished clothes. The weaving and spinning in the family home are deeply entrenched tradition and people are reluctant to change.

Freya recognises this reality and she adjusts the business focus accordingly. Young people just cannot get enough of the cloth having Margaretha's designs while Freya's catch the imagination of the older women. The team believe that they have found a winning formula. They trade with moderate success for three years, enjoying the cut and thrust of doing business and building trust in each other through fellowship.

Towards the end of the third year Freya senses, that through her engagement with the population, that all is not well in the community. It seems that the constant loss of young people is ruining the drive and enthusiasm of the community as the average age increases. Freya's parents talk more frequently of leaving Nordland for Jorvic. The level of business is starting to reduce, and Freya is considering her situation.

Harid and Margaretha decide they wish to marry and seek their parents' consent. This is freely given and the negotiations for bride price in accordance with Viking law commence.

Harid and Margaretha's news forms an idea in Freya's parent's minds and they call for a family discussion.

Gustav, with Ranveya at his side, explains, "for some time now, we have been thinking of leaving Narvik and moving to Jorvic to set up a new life in a lively community whilst we are still young enough and able to enjoy it. We intend to become traders instead of farmers, staying for a while with trading relatives in Jorvic. We intend to hand over the farm to Harid and Margaretha as soon as they are married."

This decision has already been advised to Margaretha's parents and it is agreed that no other exchange of assets is required.

Freya is immediately upset, and it shows. Ranveya, quick to spot this, tugs Gustav's sleeve, saying, "tell Freya now what you have planned for her and see if she is willing to come with us."

Gustav agrees, saying, "Freya, we want you to come with us. You said yourself that the business is reducing, and we think you could do well in Jorvic if you wish to."

Freya is somewhat mollified by this and realises there are advantages in moving. Furthermore, she has a feeling that the move may help in the fulfilment of the prophesy.

She ponders on what to do with the business and decides it would be best to hand it over to the team and let them decide what to do for the future. She explains to the team, "I have decided to go with my parents. You have been wonderful to work with. As a token of my esteem I'd like to hand over the business to you. I am sure you will continue to trade successfully even in a reducing market."

The team accept the challenge and, moved by the compliment given by Freya, start to work on a hand over plan.

The move is not to happen immediately as Harid and Margaretha's wedding needs to be organised. Gustav and Ranveya must plan and organise the transportation of their wealth, which is in the form of silver, bullion, and some gold. The plan is that they will employ a bodyguard of six heavily armed young men who also want to seek their fortune elsewhere and who find the prospect of life in Jorvic attractive. While Ranveya and Margaretha get on with planning the wedding, Gustav goes to the harbour to seek a longboat master prepared to accept a contract to transport the family, their bodyguards and their goods to Jorvic. The North Sea is a very dangerous place, it being subject to frequent violent storms which damage the ships and stress the crews. It is normal for ships to lay over in Jorvic for repairs and recuperation. This suits Gustav perfectly.

He then agrees terms of passage on a date three months ahead. This is done speedily as Gustav is highly respected in the area, especially as he has helped fund expeditions in the past.

The next three months are totally committed to Freya handing over the business, Gustav and Ranveya tidying up their affairs and handing over the farm. Overriding all plans is the wedding planning and the event itself.

As the wedding day approaches all the Viking traditional rituals of preparation from body and mind cleansing to obtaining the ceremonial sword are carried out.

The event itself proceeds without a hitch with much drinking and hilarity. It is accepted by the families and the guests that the couple are well matched. The festivities last for a week during which, in between times, Freya and her parents remove the rest of their belongings from the farm to a separate hut ready for transportation.

At the end of the week a final ceremony is carried out. With Freya standing to one side, Gustav and Ranveya stand at the door of their longhouse and beckon Harid and Margaretha to come forward. All the guests and many people from the settlement and the surrounding area have gathered to watch something quite unique in their experience.

Gustav, while holding Ranveya close to him, announces, "we wish you all to witness our handing over the farm, all implements and livestock to Harid and Margaretha for their enjoyment in perpetuity."

With that Gustav and Ranveya embrace the young couple and, standing to one side, allow them to enter the house. This is a signal for a massive outburst of applause and cheering.

When all has quietened down, Gustav again addresses the crowd, "tomorrow we leave for Jorvic with Freya, where we will share a different life with relations who are established traders there. The challenge will be enormous, but we are ready for it."

The three then move off down the path, through the crowd, to the hut which has been prepared for them to rest in before departure the following day. They are all so tired that they retire to sleep immediately.

Freya, however, is restless, fearful, and lonely. She sleeps only fitfully, dreaming about Frode and wondering where and how he is.

Next day they gather together with their six guards and move to the ship's mooring, with Gustav and the captain supervising the loading.

Just prior to sailing, everybody prays to the Gods for a safe journey. Harid and Margaretha come forward for a special embrace, as crowds gather to add their noisy farewells.

The crew casts off and the longship is rowed out to the middle of the fjord while the sail is being raised. Gustav turns to Ranveya and Freya and says,"We have a new life in front of us."

The longship heads out to sea as the waving crowd grows smaller in the distance.

As the longship gathers speed with the light wind filling the sails, the crew get on with their duties leaving the family to their own devices.

Gustav, with a serious expression on his face, comments, as they settle down for the voyage, "let us look at the scenery we have lived beside all these years and fix the memory in our minds for we shall not see the like again. Let us pray to the Gods to ask for a fair wind to Hjaltland and Jorvik."

After they have done so Gustav explains again what the family hopes to achieve. "I feel that a great adventure lies before us and we should embrace the challenge."

Freya is feeling unhappy as she knows she is leaving a world she understood and entering the unknown. She is missing Frode's company. She desperately wants to be with him; without him she feels incomplete.

She shakes her head, thinking," I am overwhelmed. Frode hear me please. I need you so much."

CHAPTER SIX

THE SEPARATION YEARS

FRODE IN THE DYFLIN AREA

Frode is standing near the prow of the longboat, gazing at the breath-taking scene. He has never seen such soft green land offset by rolling hills to the south. He is totally captivated. The longship is rowed skilfully into the dock in calm weather and is moored by crew members and loafers who hang around the dock looking to help the mooring, for a tip, of course.

The dock area is bustling with activity; ships are loading and unloading, men are shouting orders, goods of all types are being carted through the docks causing traffic jams and general chaos.

Far to one side is an extensive shipyard where diverse types of longship are being built. Dyflin has a reputation for building the finest longships in the Viking world.

Frode collects his baggage, bids the captain farewell, "thank you for a safe journey. May the Gods watch over you. Do you know of decent lodgings?"

"Try the "Liffey Inn" next to the grain warehouse over yonder." He points to a building about 200 yards from the dock. As Frode pushes his way through the milling crowd he is almost overcome by the stink, something he has never encountered before coming, as he has, from the clear clean air of Nordland. He arrives at the "Liffey Inn" and weaves his way through a raucous crowd of drinking sailors to the end of a long straight bar.

Addressing the stunningly attractive girl at the bar, "I have been told that you have accommodation. Do you have a room available?" The girl, coquettishly displaying her attractions, replies, "I am Caolinn, and we do have rooms."

Frode introduces himself to her in his soft almost musical voice, which has her heart fluttering. He agrees the price for the room for one week and pays by silver coin from Hjaltland. He had been advised to seek payment for his stories in silver, where bed and board is not on offer, as most trading costs are paid in silver within Dyflin itself. He orders a drink and a plate of fish to be taken to him in his room.

Having done so, he goes to his room to drop his baggage and to consider his next moves. Shortly afterwards Caolinn comes to deliver his meal. As she lays the wooden platter down, she appraises him directly making him uncomfortable to begin with. She is being outrageously flirtatious and Frode gives in to a wave of desire.

Later he finds himself thinking, with a sense of guilt, that he has betrayed Freya. Ashamed, he resolves that he will not allow himself to be led astray again. Having eaten his meal, he leaves the inn to explore the town. He finds out that Dyflin has a population of around four thousand and is protected by a ditch, earth rampart and a palisade. The town is occupied by Danish Vikings subscribing to a strange religion called Christianity. He decides to explore this as the idea of a single a God is quite beyond his experience.

On the south side of the river along which the town has been built, is a substantial settlement of local people. The relationship between the two communities is uneasy, but as with all traders, a compromise has been worked out. There is an increasing trend towards intermarriage between the two groups, despite the unease.

During his exploration he is made welcome by everybody and he befriends a Christian monk called Ronan who is sitting on the harbour wall talking to a group of young people. Frode stops to listen and realises he is meeting a kindred spirit. After the youngsters move away, Ronan asks Frode to join him. They tell of their backgrounds and Ronan tells Frode about a community of Christian monks living and working at a place, originally a sanctuary of St Kevin in the 6th Century, and now a monastery called Glendalough, deep in the mountains 30 miles to the south. "I am going there soon; would you like to come with me?"

Frode, excited by the prospect a new experience replies,

"In my home settlement I was a storyteller, and with the help of a friend produced plays for the children to present to the community."

Frode understands that outside Dyflin he is going to have a problem with language, so he thinks that a sojourn in Glendalough will enable him to learn the local language, to an extent that communication will not be a serious problem.

Ronan says, "I am a wanderer and storyteller too, but I also spread the word of God. We could team up and go to Glendalough together."

Frode, thinking, replies, "I agree, but I'd like to stay the week in town exploring, since I have booked a week at the "Liffey Inn"

"Let's meet at the inn in 6 days' time and go on from there." Ronan agrees.

Ronan is harbouring the idea of converting the pagan to the faith and intends to do so, thinking that Glendalough would be conducive to the purpose. He is sure that Frode could make a huge contribution to the evangelism of the monastery. After they part company, Frode spends the days at the inn listening to stories and to the music, absorbing the atmosphere. Caolinn provides him with happy, exciting company but without intimacy. Sadly, for her, she has come to realise that she is a distraction. She also senses that his heart is elsewhere.

Frode also walks around the town, talking to people, the language of Danish Vikings being very close to his own. Speaking to the Irish is more difficult but he manages to some extent by using sign language. He is helped by the fact that some of the Irish speak passable Nordic.

As promised Ronan calls at the inn for Frode. Caolinn, embraces him and bids him, "God speed and may your life be a happy one. I shall never forget you."

The pair set off through the crowded streets, heading across the river towards the south and the hills beyond, carrying a little food they had bought at the Inn. Ronan explains, "we have 30 miles to walk through the most wonderful countryside you have ever seen. In exchange for our news and stories the local people will provide us with food and shelter."

Frode is mesmerised by the soft green countryside with gentle hills and streams shimmering in the sunlight, as storm clouds gather in the distance. He stops to take in the views and comments to Ronan,"my homeland is beautiful too, but it is stark compared to this."

Then it starts to rain heavily causing Frode to wish he had brought a better cloak. Ronan, wise in the ways of the local climate, produces a second waterproofed woollen cloak from his travel bag and gives it to Frode, saying, "I thought you might not have allowed for the rain!" Thus, a bond of brotherhood is established between them.

Stopping off at two farms on the way, Frode is welcomed. As a stranger he keeps his counsel while Ronan tells Bible stories. Then Ronan turns to Frode and asks him to tell some Viking stories, which he does. After three days the two arrive in Glendalough in the morning, welcomed by the Abbot and a group of the monks. Introductions are made and once Frode and Ronan have a meal, they are invited to the Abbot's inner sanctum, a room which is austerely furnished with a single bed, a desk, a few chairs, and a corner assigned for prayer and meditation.

The Abbot asks Frode to tell him about his background and why he has come to Ireland. Frode has difficulty with the language but Ronan helps by interpreting.

Frode explains, "I am from Nordland and I am a Skald, a storyteller of Nordic tales. Like many of my people I have left my birthplace to enjoy the experiences available in the wider world and to become a travelling storyteller."

The Abbot interjects, "are you a Christian and what kind of stories do you tell?"

"No, I am not a Christian and, frankly, I know little of Christianity. Stories I tell are based on Norse history. I also pass on the news between settlements."

Frode is nervous under the penetrating gaze of the Abbot and is not sure where the questioning is leading. However, he is aware he has no option but to be honest in the views he is asked to express.

The Abbot goes on to explain, "this is a Christian House devoted to the worship of God and to the spreading of His Word. As a non-Christian you will find it impossible to be welcomed into Irish homes as the people are devout Christians."

Ronan, who has said nothing during this exchange, is watching his friend carefully and sees Frode's confusion, but continues to say nothing in deference to the Abbot's authority.

The Abbot continues, "you are welcome here as a stranger and to receive our hospitality for a little while. I will ask you to consider converting to Christianity. Without converting you will not go far in your mission, but if you do convert, you will have access everywhere in Ireland and be welcome. You will be expected to spread God's Word, but there will be no bar to your telling your Norse stories as well. Of course, you will also be expected to carry news to communities as you have done before."

At this point the Abbot is aware that Frode is confused and he decides to end the interview. In so doing he says to Frode, "you do need time to think about what I have said and then we'll have to talk a lot more. Stay with us for a while as our guest. Ronan will look after you and show you where you will sleep. He will also show you around the monastery. I hope you will find it interesting."

With that Frode and Ronan are dismissed.

Ronan takes Frode to the dormitory area and introduces him to the monk in charge.

The monk, in welcoming Frode, says, "come with me and I will show you your sleeping cell."

Frode views his cold cell with some concern as it is so small and stark, having only a simple bed, a small table, candle with holder, and chair. He is provided with eating utensils.

Ronan explains, "we live a simple life and have forsaken worldly wealth to enable us to glorify God. Leave your belongings here and I will take you on a preliminary tour. Then we will eat before I need to go to devotions. While I am in the chapel I suggest you take a rest in your cell and I will come to collect you and take you to the library where we can talk."

Frode is unsure of himself as he is in a situation beyond his experience. While he has never been very religious he understands the Norse pantheon of gods; the idea of a single God is completely beyond his comprehension. Frode, ever the opportunist, is already thinking about how he can turn the situation to his advantage. A few compromises may well be all he has to consider.

The initial tour is brief with their visiting the scriptorium, the chapels, the library, and the refectory. He likes the 100-foot-high circular observation tower.

In the refectory Frode is introduced to four monks who are eating a simple meal. He is asked to join them and during the meal Frode engages in a lively discussion, with Ronan acting as interpreter again. The monks do not have closed minds and listen intently to Frode's life story. Frode, of course, is in his element as a storyteller. The monks tell him of the work they do in the monastery, in the farm and when spreading the Word of God in the countryside.

After the meal Ronan and the other monks go to the chapel for Vespers while Frode wanders back to his cell.

Frode realises that Ronan is a gifted interpreter who has an aptitude for languages. He resolves to discuss this with Ronan when he returns.

"I'll keep an open mind and see how matters develop," he thinks as he settles down to await Ronan's return.

His mind drifts to thoughts of Freya. She is often in his thoughts anyway, but now his feelings are more intense, and he is beginning to build up fantasies about her.

He begins to doze, dreaming of Freya and what the future might hold for them.

He prays to the Nordic Gods to protect her. He asks them to tell her that he loves her, in the hope that they might regard him as important enough to do what he asks.

What he does not realise is that the Gods do regard him as important enough as they have invested so much in the idea of Frode and Freya being the leading players in the fulfilment of their prophesy. They confer to review how things are going. It is important not influence events, but they will do so if the plan is threatened.

They are a concerned that Frode may be sidetracked during his exposure to Christian teaching. They resent the intrusion the Christian teaching but are wise enough to recognise the advance of the Christian faith is unstoppable. It is best, they believe, to accept that Frode has to live in the world as it really is. They can exert influence if they need to.

Ronan returns and gently shakes him awake. "Come," he says, "we have things to do. Let's go over to the library where we can find a quiet corner and speak."

Frode, somewhat sleepily, agrees.

CHAPTER SEVEN

THE SEPARATION YEARS

FRODE AT GLENDALOUGH MONASTERY

Frode really wants to explore but he must be patient. The pace of life in the monastery is very gentle; passage of time seems not to be important.

On reaching the library they find a quiet corner and sit down. Ronan looks at Frode and seeing uncertainty in his eyes explains," I realise how strange all of this is. You have experienced things that you have never had before. If you allow me I will explain the basis of our way of life and the philosophy behind it. All I ask of you is that you keep your mind open, ask as many questions as you like and ask me to stop to allow you breathing space at any time."

Frode sits back pondering about just what he might be getting into, then answers, "alright, let me learn."

Ronan then explains what will happen and makes it clear that Frode may withdraw from the community at any time and return to Dyflyn or wander wherever the will takes him.

Ronan commences his story, immediately gaining Frode's close attention as Frode realises he is in the presence of a master storyteller. He outlines the history and purpose of the monastery.

"We here at Glendalough are devoted to spreading the knowledge of Christianity. The nature of Christianity is much more complex. If you decide to become a follower and help spread the Word by your skill at storytelling you will become an Initiate here, spending time learning from the Abbot and monks.

You also be expected to do your share of the work on the farm, and you will be required to attend the various forms of worship."

"I know you are a wanderer and cannot be expected to stay in one place for long. I doubt you will want to become a monk, so you will not need to undergo religious training. However, you have the opportunity to learn skills which will stand you in good stead in the future."

Frode, impressed with this argument, agrees to enter training. He then retires to his cell for the night, Ronan going to worship.

Next morning Frode awakes, performs his ablutions, and strolls along to the Refectory. Here he joins other monks who engage him in lively conversation, with Ronan's help in interpreting.

Many of the monks have little or no experience of life outside of the monastery and hear, with wonder and not a little suspicion, of the Norse gods and life in Nordland. In turn the monks tell him of their lifestyle and of their worship of one God. One monk is unhappy and feels threatened in the presence of a pagan, saying, "why have you come here? You are threatening our peace and communion with God!"

The other monks mutter darkly about the offence being given to a guest, but Frode is not put out and answers quietly, with Ronan interpreting, "I am an invited guest. Do you deny me the opportunity to learn of your religion and your ways? Maybe I will be convinced of your beliefs and help spread information in the communities I will visit. Who knows?"

With that mild rebuke, the tension is relieved, and the monk called Peter, smiles, and responds, "I apologise for such a display of bad manners. May I help you as much as I can?"

Frode, now more at ease, replies, "of course, I would feel privileged to learn from you as well as Ronan".

It turns out that Peter was born of Viking stock; he lived and worked in Dyflin for many years and was a wanderer before coming to Glendalough.

He is fluent in languages, gained from his wanderings, and offers to teach Frode the local language and the more widespread Gaelic. He feels drawn to Frode, because he too, is a wanderer.

The other monks are amazed, for Peter is well known for his uncompromising grumpiness.

Says one," this Frode fellow has lots of charm despite his rough dress and pagan ways. I hope he stays with us for a long time."

Another monk opines, "it will reduce our exposure to the grumbling!"

After breakfast Ronan and Frode go to a meeting with the Abbot.

The Abbot proceeds to outline the established training regime but decides that Frode needs to learn more of the local language first.

"Frode, I will outline your training plan but first I want you to spend time with Peter on language improvement. I am told that Peter has volunteered to do this. I am going to suggest this learning is achieved, not only by talking about day to day matters, but also by learning about Christ's teachings and the story of his Ministry."

Frode, liking the idea of improving his language skills quickly and under tuition, says, "I do thank you for your understanding."

The Abbot looking suitably stern makes Frode's position clear," you are now an Initiate and Ronan will be your mentor, explaining, among other things, your duties and responsibilities".

The Abbot, turning to the training regime, explains that Frode will have a tutor available to him always and he will often be joined by other Initiates.

"Frode, you will work with Peter on language, interspersing lessons with attending devotions. Furthermore, you will go on missions with Ronan. The people you visit will know you as an Initiate, and you may be accompanied by other Initiates. You must be patient, as each period of training takes time. You are free to visit and observe other parts of the monastery as your training allows and before you move there for training."

Frode, seeing a chance to influence matters, suggests, "I would like to spend time outside with Ronan as this would not only enable me to absorb the local culture but to learn Bible stories more easily."

The Abbot nods his consent and leaves the room.

Frode then goes in search of Peter and finds him in the garden. It is a beautiful, but chilly day and Frode, approaching Peter, asks, " can I sit with you and start my language lessons?"

Peter, belying his reputation for grumpiness, agrees readily, "yes please sit next to me. I will teach you to speak the local language just as your mother taught you to speak your native tongue. You will only be allowed to speak to me in Irish and If you do not know a word you must convey the meaning another way in Irish before I give you that word."

Peter is a hard taskmaster and drives Frode without mercy, telling Frode, "you are without discipline and you must gain this if you are to succeed with me."

For Frode learning mental discipline is proving frustrating but Peter is relentless in forcing Frode to concentrate.

" I must remind you that, as an Initiate, you must obey your mentors without question." Frode, while grumbling, accepts the situation.

The activities are mixed with attending the devotions in the chapel and meals with the other monks. Meals are very formal affairs which helps to instil discipline into Frode, who by Irish standards, is "a wild one."

From time to time Peter relieves the pressure by allowing Frode to visit the farm to observe its workings, but for the moment he is forbidden to become involved.

Peter promises him, "you will, in due time, have to spend time working there. I know you have farming experience which will allow you to contribute to the farm's development"

During the following six months Frode applies himself to learning languages. Peter seems has found a vocation and makes the learning process interesting and fun. Frode has a natural ability to learn languages. Towards the end of the fourth month Peter takes Frode for a walk in the garden and quietly says," you have done so well. I am impressed."

Frode, thrilled with the compliment, wonders, "I have told you that I intend leaving Ireland at some point and go over the sea to a place I believe is called Normandy. Is there any similarity between the language there and here?"

"Oh, yes. As I said earlier I spent time in Normandy."

He is overcome by the drive to go to Normandy.
"It's just a feeling," he thinks.

CHAPTER EIGHT

THE SEPARATION YEARS

FRODE GAINS NEW EXPERIENCES

Peter is secretly pleased to be able to continue teaching Frode, for he has enjoyed every moment of his time with him.

Frode happily agrees, "I want to learn, but I do need to spend time earning my keep working on the farm.

Peter says, "tell you what, -let's do a schedule covering a month at a time that allows you to learn with me, work on the farm and attend devotions."

"I agree," says Frode. He realises that the regime will be hard but feels it will be worthwhile.

Peter councils caution, saying, "we have to have the plan approved by the Abbot."

Frode, explaining, "I owe Ronan so much that I want him to know of the plan and be able to honour my promise to him that I accompany him on his missionary work"

Peter, thinking for a moment, "I see no problem there."

After evening devotions they go to the library to discuss and agree the programme. They quickly realise that they must consult the monks in charge of the farm to get their agreement and that of the Abbot.

They prepare the plan together, bringing Ronan into the discussions. Ronan helps Peter write the details down while Frode sees that writing on parchment is much more efficient than inscribing runes on pieces of wood.

A meeting is arranged with the Abbot who is given the manuscript in advance.

At the meeting the Abbot is in a genial mood, welcoming Peter and Frode warmly, "I must say that your proposal is radical. I would be proud (if that is not a sin) to have Glendalough be the force behind Frode's storytelling. Please go ahead, with my blessing."

Frode is speaking in Irish extremely well and Ronan has a quiet word with Peter.

"Would you, as a reward for his progress, allow Frode to come with me to Avoca on a short mission trip? We'd be away for about three days".

Peter, who has become a much less awkward person in recent months, ponders for a while and then, with a chuckle, says, " why not, but I want him back. We have lots of work to do."

With that Frode goes off to do his daily turn in the kitchen preparing meals.

Some days later Ronan tells Frode, "I am going to Avoca tomorrow. It's a delightful place where two rivers meet, and it is very peaceful. There I shall meet families who have become friends and seem to enjoy listening to my Bible stories. I think it would be good for you to join me. What do you think?"

Frode, with a happy mischievous smile, "yes, please! Can I dress as a Viking?"

"Not a chance; you'll wear your habit and like it!"

"Oh well" says Frode, "I am in your hands. I promise to behave myself; it's just I feel hemmed in here and I do need a bit more space"

Ronan then says, "let me go through what will happen. Avoca is more than a day's walk and so we will stay overnight with friends. You will be made welcome as I will briefly explain who you are and something of your background. You will be able to tell more of your background in your own way, which I know will intrigue our hosts. Then we will go to where the rivers meet and spend some time in quiet contemplation. With luck there will be other Christians there along with some "Brides of Christ" when we can talk and pray together."

"Who are the "Brides of Christ?" asks Frode

"They are nuns who, like us, have dedicated their lives to the worship of God and who spend time in communities helping the poor and needy. They take vows of chastity, so remember your manners!!" Frode makes no comment as he feels he must not betray his love for Freya. He remembers Caolinn for a moment, though.

As time passes it becomes clear that there is a natural affinity between them which frequently expressed in their humour.

The following day they set off. The weather is typical of late autumn. There is a strong chilly wind with clouds scudding across the sky driving a light but penetrating rain across the countryside. Both men are not fazed by this, but it is uncomfortable.

Later in the morning they find shelter in a farm building where the farmer's wife provides a warm drink and where they eat the food they have brought with them.

Later the farmer's wife invites them into the house. "Please lead us in prayer and give us your blessing."

Ronan is happy to do so and then proceeds to tell the story of one of Christ's miracles, that of turning water into wine.

"Smacks of witchcraft" Frode jokes to Ronan, we could make a fortune out of that!"

Ronan is not amused, muttering something about God shall not be mocked.

Frode realises that he must be careful as to what he says as he realises that Ronan takes his vocation very seriously indeed.

"I am sorry I was irreverent; it's just that I am new to this and it's fundamentally different from the beliefs I was brought up with."

Ronan just nods and strides on. Frode resolves to be quiet and hopes that Ronan will cease to be annoyed.

As they approach the outskirts of the tiny settlement of Avoca Ronan says, "we are visiting my friends, the O'Donnell family."

As they continue walking, Ronan explains that the family has two teenage sons who will want to know all about Nordland and the Viking way of life.

"However, do not be drawn into discussions about Norse Gods. It's not long since they converted from paganism so they could be confused."

The tension between them evaporates.

They reach the small thatched house which is no bigger than a large hut. They are made welcome, with Ronan introducing Frode to the family. The family is poor, the house having little furniture. It has a sleeping area, not unlike the home Frode was brought up in, and a central fire in which native turf is slowly burning.

They sit down to a simple meal after Ronan has said Grace. The two boys are eager to get on with the meal so that they can hear the story. Mindful of Ronan's earlier advice Frode, at the end of the meal asks permission to tell a story. "I am happy to tell stories of my life in Narvik. However, then I was a pagan. I do not wish to undermine your faith."

The parents respond, "we are happy to hear you speak and we are sure that Ronan will ensure our minds are not poisoned. We can regard your story as a history lesson."

Frode gathers everyone around him and proceeds,

"I will tell you of a group of children who banded together to write and perform little plays for the people of our village. We had long cold dark periods where we lived far to the north; the plays were a way keeping occupied and it worked quite well, I think."

Frode tells his story, accepting constant interruptions from his audience.

Later, Mr O'Donnell is so pleased that in offering them overnight hospitality, in the manner of the Irish, he says, "in a couple of days come back and we can go to our neighbours where they are holding a ceilidh."

Frode, who has never heard of a ceilidh asks Ronan, "what's a ceilidh? Ronan replies, "it's a party with lots of music, dancing and fun. Wait and see; you will love it."

In the morning they breakfast and, after bidding farewell to their hosts they set off for Avoca.

As they walk down the hill on a wild and windy day, Frode is assailed by doubts about where his life is leading. He is not at ease with the rigid sedentary life at Glendalough and wonders what to do. He is not keen on sharing his doubts with Ronan. As they come to the place where the two rivers meet they are greeted warmly by monks and nuns who arc meeting there. Fortunately, the weather has improved enough to enable all there to relax and talk. Frode, bereft of female company, drifts over to a group of nuns. He interrupts their lively chatter, but they are not impressed with him. It seems his rough appearance frightens them.

Frode shrugs his shoulders and wanders back to Ronan and a group of monks who are debating some point of Christian doctrine. He mutters darkly in Ronan's ear, "and you told me to keep my hands to myself! It would be easier to make love to a stone."

Ronan cannot contain himself, replying through a storm of giggles," met your match, eh?" Frode is furious and strides off in a huff.

The other monks are unhappy with the interruption and tell Ronan," concentrate, this is a serious debate." This he does, but very reluctantly.

Both Frode and Ronan feel that the visit to Avoca has not been a rewarding experience and decide to return to the O'Donnell's farm.

On arriving at the farm, they settle in with family again and go to the ceilidh.

The singing and dancing and eating there reminds Frode of his life in Narvik. His mood lightens immediately and says to Ronan, "I have missed this so much. I am beginning to feel that, with the experience in Avoca, and the jollity here, I am not suited to the monastic life. To me it has become dull and restraining." He looks at Ronan, "you and the monks at Glendalough are so generous and hospitable that I feel churlish when I think this way; it is so ungrateful."

In reply Ronan slaps him on the shoulder saying, "let's just enjoy the evening and we can talk on the way back tomorrow."

Everybody has a wonderful time and on retiring to the barn to sleep, Frode bids Ronan "good night" saying, "this has been like home."

He turns over to go to sleep and after a while and when asleep he sees an image of Freya appearing before him. She beckons to him and, as he approaches her she whispers," you have not forgotten me, have you?" He cries out, "no, no. I love you to distraction!".

Ronan shakes him awake, "are you all right. What was that all about?" he enquires.

Frode replies, shakily," yes, I think so."

Ronan, however, is very intrigued and pushes Frode for more information," who is she then that she can cause you such distress?"

Frode feels he must share his thoughts and for a while he tells Ronan of the childhood friendship with Freya, the plays, and the prophesy.

Ronan, at the end of the tale indicates, "thanks for trusting me. I have a clearer insight into your soul which I felt was a little troubled. Let us pray for guidance and talk again during our return journey."

They pray and then go back to sleep. Frode's sleep is, despite the prayer, unsettled.

In the morning they share breakfast with the O'Donnell family and then bid farewell to the family and their friends.

The weather is sunny and quite warm.

Ronan reminds Frode of his pledge to tell his story, "after all you are supposed to be a storyteller; so, come on, prove it"

Frode, amused by the challenge from his closest friend, proceeds to tell his tale. Ronan is entranced and when Frode comes to the point where he leaves Narvik for Dyflin he stops. "I am not sure where I go from here".

Ronan, with a serious expression on his face, says, "I have something to say to you. Please let's take a break and sit down on the bank of this stream. "You say you are not sure about where you go from here. May I give you my opinion, from someone who has become your friend?"

Frode nods his acceptance.

Ronan continues," it has become obvious that you will never become a monk. Remember that the Abbot told you that you could leave Glendalough whenever you wish. I believe the prophesy and I am not so prejudiced as to regard other Gods as being of no account. It seems to me your destiny with Freya will be fulfilled if you embrace it completely. I strongly advise you to do so. Being converted to Christianity will be a help, not a hindrance."

Ronan pauses and waits for Frode to react. Frode broods for a while and then exclaims, "so if you are right, and I have to believe you are, what do you suggest I do now?"

"I suggest you move on to wherever your destiny leads you. I believe the sojourn at Glendalough is part of the preparation and that you have some more time there yet."

They rise, and start walking again at a stiff pace and enjoy the peace of the countryside. Soon they reach Glendalough and are welcomed back by the Brothers. Ronan immediately goes to the chapel to pray while Frode goes to meditate in his cell.

Frode believes that, while it is time to move on, he has a duty to repay the generosity shown to him and thinks that, during a meeting with the Abbot, he should offer to work on the farm for a while.

Ronan returns, and they go to the Refectory for a meal.

Other monks are eager to hear about the visit to Avoca and of news picked up by them on their travels. Ronan is happy to do so. As Ronan tells of their experiences, Frode is again struck by the thought that this life is not for him. He thinks, "this life is mundane and lacking in adventure. However, I must repay the generosity shown to me."

The following day Frode seeks a meeting with the Abbot. Ronan declines the invitation to join them as he feels that the issues that Frode faces are intensely personal.

The Abbot, meeting with Frode in the privacy of his room, introduces the discussion by saying," you seem intensely troubled, my friend. Let us pray and then I'll hear your confession" They do this and Frode reveals his doubts during his confession.

Frode speaks at length, holding nothing back while the Abbot listens intently.

When Frode has finished he feels that a huge burden has been lifted. He has found it easier to talk to the Abbot because of the discussions he has had with Ronan.

The Abbot orders a light meal, provided, and delivered by Ronan. Ronan says nothing but looks at Frode and gives a smile of encouragement before he departs.

The Abbot says, "Frode, I said to you that you can leave Glendalough whenever you wish. Notwithstanding your pagan background you have embraced the Christian faith and I believe that God will support you in your quest to see the prophesy fulfilled. I am delighted by your wish to repay our care by working on the farm and I gladly accept this."

Frode asks," how do you suggest I go from here?"

"Why don't you spend a year here during which time you can continue your language lessons with Peter, work on the farm and travel outside from time to time with Ronan and other monks."

During the next few months Frode spends time working hard on the farm, bring his own knowledge to bear.

One day Ronan, when walking through the farm hails Frode, "come, take a rest and walk with me!"

Frode delighted to have a chance to speak with his friend in private readily agrees.

Frode, when they are walking some way from the other farm labourers, has a desire to share the complete prophesy with Ronan, to expand on what he had already shared with him

"Ronan, as you know I have been the subject a prophesy made when I was a child. I am uncertain about what is happening, and I am not sure what to do. Can you help?"

Ronan, who by this time has a good knowledge of Frode's personality, and something of the prophesy already, agrees, saying, "please tell me."

Frode tells Ronan the whole story of what the prophesy is and how it came about.

They continue walking across a field on a bright frosty late January morning. For once there is no rain or wind in prospect.

"What a perfect setting for thinking about serious and important topics. Let's sit it in that, pointing at a building on the edge of the field, for a while," says Ronan. They walk on towards the building.

After a little while Ronan speaks. "I believe you are one to create the new dynasty with Freya. What is happening to you is in preparation for this. No-one can avoid their destiny, although only a few are privileged to have an awareness of it."

Going on, while Frode is listening intently, "I believe Freya is aware of what is happening as her intuition should be more finely tuned than yours. I think, wherever she is, she is following a path to the same destination as you.

He pauses to gather his thoughts, then continues, "it seems to me that your destiny is to help spread the Viking culture through mixing peacefully with other races, while abandoning the brutality of the raiding your people have been carrying out."

Frode, at last, sees through the mist in his mind that has caused him to be confused.

He stands up, embraces his friend, exclaiming, "thank you for being so honest. Whatever happens to me in the future I shall never forget you. They then continue their walk back to the monastery.

When they reach the monastery, they are called to a meeting in the refectory. Here the Abbot explains to the monks that he has received disturbing news.

He declares," Word is about that the native Irish are getting restive over the Viking control of Dyflyn and the surrounding area. High King Brian Baru, while constantly warring with petty kings, has decided to try to oust the Vikings and their king of Dyflyn once and for all".

He goes on, "the news also indicates that it will be some months before battle can be joined, so we must review our defences and strengthen them. Brother David, I put you in charge. Please let me have a report on improvements within the week."

The Abbot speaks to Frode one day. "It is now time that you accept the Christian faith before you leave us. The world is moving rapidly to the worship of the one true God."

Frode seeing the sense of this, "I agree."

The Abbot and two other monks arrange Frode's baptism one week hence.

On the appointed day all the monks and some of the laity gather in the chapel and Frode is baptised according to the rites of the monastery of Glendalough.

On completion of the ceremony, the Abbot, to the loud acclaim of all present, gives Frode an illuminated parchment Baptismal Certificate, prepared by the monks of the Scriptorium.

Frode retires to his cell to consider his future actions. He decides that his plan centres on heading for the Viking settlement at Waterford in the south.

Eventually news of a big battle at Clontarf, just north of Dyflin, comes through. In the battle, although King Brian Baru is killed, Dyflyn forces of the Vikings are defeated. Dyflyn is occupied but little killing of civilians or property damage is done. It is learned that the Irish have exacted tribute from the Vikings and that their forces have withdrawn, but not before it is agreed that there be greater integration of the peoples.

All of this takes place after Frode has decided to move. The Abbot allows him to leave, suspecting the situation encourages Frode to go forward with his quest.

Certainly, Frode feels that he must move on to reach out for pastures new.

On the day he leaves all the monks pray with him and they all gather at the gate singing a Te Deum Laudamus to wish him well, the Abbot having made a concession for this to be done. Ronan decides to walk some way with him as he heads south.

By the banks of a fast- flowing stream with a plank bridge the two friends stop. They eat a meal drawn from the week's supplies that Frode has taken, drinking the cool water from the stream.

On finishing the meal, the two men stand up and, with not a little emotion they embrace, agreeing never ever to forget their friendship. With that Frode crosses the bridge and Ronan turns back towards Glendalough. They each turn to give a brief wave before going their separate ways.

Frode, with a new sense of purpose, strides out confidently towards Wexford.

CHAPTER NINE

THE SEPARATION YEARS

FREYA IN JORVIC

After passing into the Northern Sea the voyage is uneventful during which they are joined by two other long ships. Freya, despite trying to downplay her charms, draws the attention of some of the crew, including the captain. Gustav is in a difficult position as he cannot afford to alienate the crew. However, he has a quiet word with their security guards, asking them, "please make it clear that attentions are unwelcome." They agree, and the problem is dealt with before it becomes serious.

Freya, however, is a little upset as she feels she can take care of herself and sulks for a while, much to Gustav's puzzlement. Privately, she must admit she enjoyed the attention.

Ranveya, as always wise in the way of women, "don't worry, Gustav, she'll come around. Just leave her be."

The three longships arrive at the island of Hjaltland on a fine summer's evening. As usual there are a few days rest before moving on. Gustav, his family, and the guards are looked after by Bjorn (who had looked after Frode when he was there). Without realising the connection, Bjorn, after a pleasant supper on the first night speaks at length about a young man called Frode who had passed through and how he had enthralled the local families telling his stories. His daughter, Fiona, speaks of him, too, but in a way that causes Freya to wonder if there had been any relationship between them. She decides that there had not been time but, none the less, she becomes moody which Ranveya observes, "Freya, stop it, you should not be jealous!"

Freya retorts acidly," of course I am. I miss Frode so much and I worry that, despite the prophesy, we'll never meet again."

Ranveya decides to say no more.

Gustav, planning to take advantage of the days before sailing on, visits the owner of a large successful trading business to see at first hand the kind of operation he would like to set up. Freya joins him as she now has a taste for business and is thinking of asking her father if he would consider allowing her to join him in his business venture. She decides to wait until matters develop in Jorvic.

Both feel that the time spent has been instructive.

A few days later they re-embark and set sail. This time the ship crosses a dangerous route between the islands and the mainland, notorious for violent currents. They all spend a miserable day making the crossing and, thanks to the skill of the crew, and prayers to Sjofn, safely reach calmer waters.

On the way south, the ship calls in briefly at port on the north-east of the mainland where the captain and some of the crew have relatives, but they do not stay long. Some of the crew stay behind, their places being taken by local young men of Danish Viking background.

They help Gustav understand most of the differences in the cultures between Nordic and the Danish Vikings of Jorvic.

The voyage to Jorvic takes another two days in atrocious weather conditions, which, despite it being high summer, are not that unusual.

Gustav's contact in Jorvic is the family of distant relatives, Dag, his wife Astrid, their son Hakon and their daughter Helga. They are long established successful traders and Gustav is hoping they can assist him and his family to set up their own business.

Gustav, immediately on landing, reports to the port and settlement governing bodies who provide them with temporary accommodation and secure storage for their goods and other property.

The guards help unload the ship and transport Gustav's goods to the secure store. Gustav pays them off with a handsome bonus and wishes them well in the future. Two of the guards are offered jobs at the secure store which they accept.

After moving into the temporary hut, Gustav, Ranveya and Freya spend time setting up in the hut, exploring the settlement and looking for permanent accommodation.

They find Jorvic to be crowded, frantically busy and overwhelming. Gustav, as they walk towards the centre of the settlement, comments, "this is a raucous noisy place. I do hope we can settle here for a while."

Ranveya says nothing, but Freya is excited by all that is going on around her; all the shouting, arguing, trading, vendors vying for trade in foodstuffs, jewellery, livestock, and myriad other commodities. It is lively, colourful, and malodorous. Freya thinks, "apart from the smell this suits me well."

A couple of days after their arrival Gustav sets out alone to find Dag's place of business. The first person he asks immediately points to a substantial building by the quay. He goes to the building and in passing through the main entrance he sees a well- built man, of obvious wealth wearing fine woollen clothes sitting in an open area and talking earnestly with a group of men, who are also well dressed.

Gustav waits until the group finish their business and then approaches the man whom he thinks is Dag.

"Are you Dag?", he asks.

"I am" comes the reply," and who are you?"

"I am Gustav recently arrived from Narvik and propose to stay here for a while before moving on to Normandy. I believe I am distantly related to you."

Dag, is very suspicious as he has met people making this claim before to seek money from him' looks Gustav in the eye saying," why should I believe you? Prove it!"

In reply Gustav says," I cannot prove it but if I tell of my family background in Narvik maybe you will accept the family link."

Dag, intrigued by Gustav's exuding an air of confidence and wealth, points to a tavern across the way," alright, let's go over there and you can tell me your tale and why you have come to see me."

The two enter the tavern where, despite the noise, they find a quiet corner. It is evident that Dag's position in the community commands respect and no-one intrudes upon them while they talk.

Dag orders two large jugs of ale, looks at Gustav, saying, "convince me!"

Gustav, succinctly outlining his family history, refers to families leaving Narvik to settle elsewhere.

"My grandfather often told the story about part of my family resettling in Jorvic about seventy years ago and word came back that they had established a trading business there. I believe that was your family."

Dag remains impassive. Gustav seems to want nothing material from him. He is also almost certain that Gustav's story is true, yet he wants to consider matters.

After what Gustav considers an inordinate length of time, Dag responds," It is true we originated in Narvik. Now what is it you want from me?"

Gustav, not being used to being in a subordinate position, swallows his pride and replies," I have always been a farmer but in leaving Narvik I seek to branch out into trading on my own, learning here with your help and then establishing a business in Normandy or Brittany.

Dag impressed, with Gustav's bearing and background decides that he has nothing to lose by helping. In fact, he sees an advantage in having another arm to his business.

With that in mind, he stands up to his full height of over six feet. Gustav stands up also and, at six feet tall as well, meets Dag eye to eye. The traditional Viking establishing the meeting of equals is met.

Dag, smiling broadly, "come with your family to have a meal with us tonight. I will send a servant to collect you. Where are you living?"

Gustav describes the location and Dag says, "I am sure my man will find you, but it would help if you pinned a large piece of coloured cloth by your door.

With that they leave the tavern, going their separate ways in driving rain. Gustav yells, "is it always like this?"

Dag, roaring with laughter, shouts back, "of course."

Gustav arrives back at his hut, soaked through but full of optimism. He tells Ranveya and Freya of events of the day.

Both ladies are caught up in Gustav's enthusiasm and go off to prepare for the evening. Gustav places a piece of red cloth on the door.

A few hours later there is a call from outside, "is Gustav there?" to which Gustav replies," yes-coming"

The guide, having the physique of a warrior, leads them off to the other side of town, pushing his way through throngs of people. Freya thinks," does this town ever sleep? I am not sure I can cope." She sees from her mother's expression that she is unsure as well. However, Freya, being a very pragmatic person, turns to her mother saying, above the hubbub of the crowds, "let's make our mark. We are not easily intimidated!"

Eventually the arrive at an imposing wattle and daub building standing apart from other nearby buildings.

The guide ushers them into an imposing room which is well furnished in the simple way of Vikings.

Dag comes into the room with his wife Gudrun and son Hakon, introducing them. Immediately the atmosphere becomes relaxed as everybody chatters with each other prior their being provided with a meal of several types of fish and bread. The company is at ease with Gustav and Ranveya telling of life in Nordland, while Dag and Gudrun tell of what is happening in Jorvic.

Freya becomes bored and spends time with the two large dogs which are roaming around freely. They are actually guard dogs but when "off duty" are amenable to human attention. In fact, Freya is missing Frode even more keenly as her life has become disrupted by moving from Narvik.

She feels intensely that she needs Frode by her side.

The men then leave to go down to Dag's trading building to discuss business while the women stay to talk. Freya tells of the business she ran in Narvik, explaining how she introduced vibrant colours into the cloth she wove and the wool she spun. She found her dark mood lifting as she spoke of the way the women of Narvik were thrilled to enjoy the change from the dullness of their clothes.

Gudrun picking up the idea, exclaims," we have a total lack of colour here. It must be our culture. But I am sure you could change all that"

Freya points out," I do not have the capital to set up a business from scratch"

Gudrun, looking thoughtful, replies," Let me think on this. I am sure there is an answer. The thought of your bringing some colour to the women of the community is a compelling one. How about we meet tomorrow and discuss it?"

Freya, smiling broadly, "oh, yes please?"

With that they arrange to meet outside the jewellery workshop next to Dag's office the next day.

They continue to chat until the men return.

Dag says, "Gustav and I reckon there is an advantage in our working together and we are going to meet tomorrow so that Gustav can see how my trading business works. Then we can see if we can make arrangements.

Gudrun then explains what she and Freya have in mind. Just before they are escorted home, Gustav, turning to Dag and Gudrun, "thank you for inviting us into your home and for your generosity. Our collaboration will be fruitful." They then take their leave.

Dag puts his arm round Gudrun's waist, "I do believe we have exciting and profitable times ahead." Gudrun nods in agreement as they retire for the night.

CHAPTER TEN

THE SEPARATION YEARS

FREYA'S FAMILY IN JORVIC

Dag, Hakon and Gustav meet in Dag's trading offices and warehouse located adjacent the main harbour moorings. The area is thronged with people all rushing about intent on their own business. Just occasionally there are small groups of people gossiping or talking business.

Dag acquired this prime location by buying out the earlier trader who had to sell up through ill health.

Dag tells Gustav, "I own six longships and charter others as I require them. There is a thriving market in ship charters here. Right now, I have my longships at sea with three other charters to enable me always to maintain my business"

Hakon interjects," I fix the charters and hope one day to have my own charter fleet. Meantime I assist my father in the business."

The men then go on a tour of the warehouse which by any standards is huge, the length of twenty longships and fifteen wide.

Gustav is amazed by the variety of goods in the warehouse, ranging from bales of different fabrics, silver goods, farming implements, building materials and many, many others.

Dag admits to being a leading slave trader, supplying slaves to businesses and wealthy homes in Jorvik and the surrounding area. The slave trade is carried out in an area in a sparsely populated part of the port.

Gustav does not approve of slaving but does not make any comment.

Dag explains that although he is a trader he only works within the local population. The real trading is done by the captain of each longship who is a totally trusted and experienced trader who has free hand in finalising deals. His reward is a share of the profits, with the crew also being paid that way.

Dag looks at Gustav (who has been puzzled, never having come across this method of payment before) grins and says, "there is no better incentive for a man than to be offered a share in the profits from a trading voyage.

My ships trade with settlements in Dyflin, Normandy, Brittany and Cornwall. Some even go up to the Baltic sea.

When Viking raiders capture slaves, I am one of the first to be offered them for selling on. That is very profitable, and I have a reputation for offering healthy and well-fed slaves. There is a steady market in slaves here".

They agree that Gustav spends time in the warehouse to learn what commodities are being traded, where they come from and where they go to. In the process he will learn the means of the control of the flow of goods. He will also make some voyages to observe the process of bargaining for goods and slaves.

He is aware that he will need to spend up to two years learning the business.

Having decided on the learning role that Gustav is going to play, Gustav returns to his family and, over a meal, explains, "I worked out a plan with Dag and Hakon which will allow me to learn the trading business over the next couple of years. It will also entail my going on voyages probably to Dyflin and Normandy."

"Dag has the idea that we could expand the business into Normandy and we agreed that when I go to Normandy I would do some research whilst there."

Ranveya looks very worried and says," Gustav, I am not happy about our being separated, especially when you are on voyages which we know are dangerous. Much as I want you to succeed, I do feel concerned."

Gustav, laughing, "I thought of that and Dag agreed that it would be a good idea for you to come with me.

Freya, with a troubled expression, "what about me?"

"Think about the opportunity you have here!" responds Gustav."

"Hmmm", thinks Freya, her mind immediately thinking…

CHAPTER ELEVEN
THE SEPARATION YEARS

FREYA CONSIDERS SETTING UP HER BUSINESS

As arranged Freya meets Gudrun outside Dag's offices and, since it is a warm, sunny day, they decide to move away from the noisy bustle of people and retire to an open area to sit on the grass.

Gudrun opens their conversation," please tell me all about your business in Narvik. It sounds a good story."

Freya takes time to gather her thoughts and then proceeds to describe in detail of how she, and her friends, with her father's backing, set up and developed a clothes-making business. During Freya's story Gudrun poses searching questions. The story takes a long time in the telling, so they return to Gudrun's house for lunch.

During the meal Freya has a flash of inspiration. She is dressed in the style of local women, a plain light brown woollen dress with a shawl wrapped round her shoulders of similar colour. "It's all very dull," she thinks. With a big smile she turns to Gudrun and says," Why should I not dress in the bright coloured dresses I used to make and wear? I can make stylish ones for richer people. We will need to check, but I believe there must be a good- sized market in and around Jorvic.

Gudrun, impressed with Freya's thinking, immediately agrees and Freya goes home to change. She had brought a selection of dresses with her from Narvik.

When Freya returns, she is wearing a stunning woollen shift type dress with a simple waist tie and no adornment. As the weather is quite cold she has complimented the dress with a woollen shawl. Her legs are covered with woollen leggings and boots to mid-calf. To complete a very attractive appearance she has let her hair down to below her shoulders. She has been aware of the stares of people as she walks from her house, proving to her that walking in her dresses is the best way of advertising her wares.

The blend of reds, yellows and greens takes Gudrun's breath away. Immediately she reaches out, embraces Freya and declares," you are looking wonderful and the dress is like nothing I have ever seen. You must go ahead."

Freya, however, sees the problem in that she has not enough money to set up. Her face betrays her sadness at an opportunity missed.

Gudrun already knows the problem as it was alluded to the previous evening, and has resolved, that if Freya can convince her that she has a viable business proposition, she will offer to invest in the business.

"Freya, I believe you have outlined a marvellous business idea and I'd like to discuss with you my helping you financially. We can agree on how to do it later."

Freya brightens up immediately and is happy to agree," I am sure it would work as I feel we get on so well. Can we work this out between ourselves?"

"Oh yes, we can. I have independent means and Gustav does not interfere with my financial activities. In fact, we work well together, giving each other comments on all subjects we discuss, including business. He will always give advice if we ask for it. I even see his providing all sorts of things like cloth and dyes. More of that later!"

"Now, I have an idea. Do you have a dress of high quality and style which would fit me? You see, I think we should dress up and walk about Jorvic displaying the dresses. If we watch reactions, as you have just done, we can see if there appears to be a market."

Freya, jumping up and down like an excited schoolgirl, is thrilled by Gudrun's support and enthusiasm, exclaiming, "yes, yes, let's go to my house now. I have just the dress in mind and I am sure it will fit you. If not, I can adjust it."

They set off across town, paying close attention to what the women are wearing, noting that so many were wearing dull working clothes. This makes Freya wonder if the women would ever want coloured dresses, but Gudrun indicates, as they crossed a muddy street crowded with animals and children, all making a fearful din, "surely women are always attracted by colour. Just introduce colour into the material used in weaving the wool and I believe you will really do well."

On arriving at Freya's house Freya introduces Gudrun to her mother.

"May I leave you to chat while I go to find a suitable dress for Gudrun?"

While Freya is away Gudrun and Ranveya discuss Freya's ideas and about Gudrun's thinking of investing.

Ranveya says," Freya has always been imaginative and made an enormous success of her business in Narvik. She understands business, having learned from her father."

Freya returns carrying a woollen dress a full-length flared skirt, a bodice with plain neck and long sleeves. The skirt has panels in red and gold colours, the bodice contrasted with red and green. The sleeves are in green.

Gudrun is very impressed, "my goodness, you could change things here with a range of dresses like that."

Gudrun is eager to try it on and promptly does so.

As it is tight in the waist, Freya exclaims, "alteration will not be a problem. Give me till tomorrow."

Gudrun, on leaving to go home, turns at the entrance to the house and asks," Freya, are you willing to allow me to provide some of the finance to enable you to start the business?"

Freya responds, her eyes shining with enthusiasm, "yes, I do have money to put into the business too, but not enough."

Gudrun, feeling as much enthusiasm as Freya, "give me a couple of days to do some thinking and research. I'll be in touch then."

They bid farewell and Freya goes to the rear of the hut to carry out the alterations to the dress. She is so excited that Ranveya asks her to calm down.

Meanwhile Gudrun is wandering about the settlement thinking and observing. When she reaches home, she finds Gustav there.

"Gustav, I have been speaking with Freya and she has a wonderful business proposition I would like to invest in."

Gustav, who is always supportive of Gudrun's ideas says," I thought something was being hatched. Go for it and good luck. I would be happy to trade with you in the provision of any goods you need-at the right price, of course!"

Gudrun, with a mischievous grin," Now we will see just how good you are!"

Both chuckle good naturedly in the manner of a couple completely at ease with each other.

CHAPTER TWELVE

THE SEPARATION YEARS

FREYA SETS UP HER BUSINESS

Two days after their meeting Gudrun and Freya meet again to check the fitting of the dress. It fits perfectly. Freya puts on another dress which is simple in style but in light brown interspersed with flashes of red and black.

Gudrun agrees," we need to research by travelling around talking to prospective customers.

Freya, not losing any of her enthusiasm, suggests, "let's go walk about together and see what happens. It would be fun to stroll around and see the reactions,"

"That's an excellent idea, Freya. Let's go."

The two of them stroll around the streets keeping to the more affluent sections of the settlement, drawing stares and complimentary comments. They experience some non-complimentary ones as well, mainly casting doubts about their morals.

On return to Freya's house they agree that they need much more information on where and what they can sell, but they already feel that business will be viable.

Gudrun says, "I shall start tomorrow visiting friends and contacts and I shall wear this dress to give an indication of what we can produce."

Freya, agrees, "I will work out what we need to get started. I need to find people who are willing to work for us in their own homes. Spinners, weavers, dressmakers, and the like. I intend that I will employ a fuller to dye the wools while I work closely with him to control the colours and the consistence of shades, which is difficult to achieve. I will need to find a shearman to finish the cloth before it goes out to the dressmakers."

In the ensuing weeks Gudrun visits friends and contacts, reporting back to Freya each evening. Eventually Gudrun says to Freya," I have found very favourable responses, but they want to know prices, so we'll need to work on that."

Freya responds, "right let's talk it through and you advise me. We are not ready yet as I am still working the details of outworkers."

Shortly afterwards Freya, having met many people willing to accept work from her, decides that there are four people who would appear to be able to produce the standard of work required. They are working in three houses and have two looms and four spinning machines.

Freya, looking thoughtful," I found that the looms were very old and not suited to the work. I have indicated that we would be prepared to supply them. I don't think that we should go further until we see how things develop."

She continues," I think I have found a fuller and shearman and I will be speaking to them over the next few days."

"I have also talked to Dag who has given me the name of a carpenter who makes all sorts of things, including looms if we provide him with the designs we need. In addition, Dag can arrange the supply of wool, threads, silks and dyes and has offered reasonable prices."

Gudrun notices that Freya has said nothing about dressmakers, asks," what about dressmakers?"

"Ah, there I have a problem. I have not found any I feel I can use."

Gudrun says," hold on. One of my friends has friends in the nearby Saxon community. As you know the two communities are getting along together much better these days. I will explore this avenue."

Freya is happy to agree, exclaiming, " yes, because we cannot move until we find the answer. Nor can we price our dresses yet." I have decided that I want to persuade my father to extend our house so that I can have a work room where I can make up the dyes and dye the wool. Here I can examine the work coming in and supervise the dressmaking"

Both, while full of enthusiasm, realise that they need to be patient and thorough in their planning.

Freya's father is agreeable to having the workshop constructed and Hakon, who is looking to find something to do that is different takes on the task.

Gudrun feels that Freya should join her in her meeting with the Saxons and, since Hakon is working on the workshop, she should not miss the opportunity.

They travel by horse and cart, which Dag has lent them. They carry sample dresses to show the dressmakers they meet, to a Saxon village 5 miles to the west of Jorvic, which supports a farming community.

As they travel through wild, beautiful country of rolling hills and myriad streams they talk about plans and their ambitions. On arriving at the village, they are surrounded by hordes of chattering children in welcome. The village has none of the squalor of Jorvic.

Freya, who has never seen a Saxon village before is struck by the similarity of the buildings' construction to Viking structures, using the same materials of wood and thatch. They are greeted by the village chief, Cedric, and his wife Odella, who live in a large building known as a hall which serves the same purpose as the Viking longhouse. The layout of the buildings is not as formal as a Viking settlement.

Cedric enquires, "what is the purpose of your visit?"

Freya explains," May we thank you for your warm welcome? We are setting up a business in Jorvic and we need to find skilled dressmakers. There are none in Jorvic having the right skills."

Then Odella interjects, "tell me what your plans are."

Freya answers by speaking of the plan to introduce dresses having vivid colours and style to the wealthy part of the population. She excuses herself, goes outside and returns with a sample dress. The chief's wife, catching her breath, exclaims, "I have never seen anything so beautiful in my life. I thought we had the imagination in our society to produce lovely clothes, but we have never, to my knowledge, done anything like this. It's absolutely stunning."

Freya then says, "we are told that you have women here with great skills and we would like your permission to see if any would be willing to work for us from their homes here."

The chief, Cedric, after consulting Odella, responds, "we have no objection provided you treat the women fairly."

"That is understood and a sensible requirement which we would honour."

Gudrun, meantime, is looking closely at the women of the village, seeing that they are better dressed than their equivalent in Jorvic.

The chief invites them to stay with them while they meet the village dressmakers, which the chief promises to bring together the next day. He will ask them to bring samples of their work.

There are lots of comings and goings to the chief's hall, with their being introduced to many of the visitors. The atmosphere is friendly and relaxed, far more than they expected.

Gudrun takes the opportunity to whisper "this village is cleaner than Jorvic and seems very prosperous. There must be very skilled dressmakers here when you see the quality of workmanship."

Freya whispers back, "yes, but the designs are poor. This is where we have the opportunity. We could even sell our dresses here if we adjust the designs to suit the local customs!"

After an evening of talk, storytelling, and eating everybody settles down for the night. Freya is surprised by the similarity of the range of food eaten by Vikings and Saxons. She wonders if the two races were one in the past. Both Freya and Gudrun feel they have been treated as honoured guests. They are full of optimism.

Next morning, Cedric invites the three dressmakers to meet Freya and Gudrun. They are shown the sample dresses Freya and Gudrun have brought and, in turn, the dresses made by the local women are examined.

The five women and Odella talk about the workmanship and what Freya expects. She has already decided that the three dressmakers are skilled enough to satisfy her demands and now realises that she could have solved the major problem.

Freya asks," are you willing to work for me, making dresses to my designs and materials? I do not wish to interfere with your existing work, but I hope you would be able to cope with the additional work."

Two agree that they would work with Freya, subject to agreement on payment. The third declines; Freya thinks that she does not want to work for a Viking.

Further discussions lead to agreement on payment and other issues. Taking their leave, Freya says," thank you all for meeting us. Once we have set things up in Jorvic, we'll meet again."

The farewells are cordial and full of promise for a very successful venture.

On their return to Jorvic, Freya and Gudrun agree that Freya will concentrate on getting the equipment in place at the outworkers and in her workshop. Dag has had the looms built and Hakon has had the workshop extension completed.

Freya calls in to see Dag and Hakon, "thank you both for doing so much work for me, I do appreciate it very much. Dag, can we discuss and agree terms for you to supply wool, silks, threads and dyes?"

"No problem. Please give me details and quantities and I'll see to it. If you wish you can store materials in my warehouse."

At that moment Gustav comes in and giving Freya a big hug, says, "I'm off to Normandy tomorrow and mother is coming with me. Dag wants me to explore the possibility of setting up a trading business there as an offshoot of this one. We are very excited. It's good to see that your plans are coming to fruition. Good luck. We expect to be away for about two months."

When all matters are decided Freya becomes less sure of herself and wanders off to find solitude by the river. Despite the cold biting wind sweeping in from the east, she stays out in the open under a large tree. It is not as cold as Narvik, but it is damp as against the crisp dryness of Narvik.

She is assailed by her need to be with Frode; she has been suppressing thoughts of him whilst concentrating on the business. She realises that her purpose in life cannot be running a business or doing anything else without Frode by her side. She is impatient, but she accepts that to meet her destiny, the Gods have devised trials and tribulations for her to conquer. She assumes that Frode is experiencing something similar.

Nonetheless, in a fit of lonely despair she prays to her Gods, "please, oh, please keep Frode safe and dream to him that I love him to distraction and miss him terribly. Surely it cannot be long before we meet again."

The Gods, in their own mysterious ways, allow Freya the comfort of sensing that Frode is well, but no more than that.

Being so comforted, she returns to her new workshop and arranges the equipment layout before spending time listening to Gustav telling of the plans he has when he reaches Normandy.

The next few weeks are frantically busy for Freya.

She only sees Gudrun occasionally when Gudrun visits to report on responses to her market research. Researches show that the market is limited. Freya feels that this will be the challenge she needs.

She is beginning to understand that this business is only a passing phase in her life, perhaps a form of training for the future. She feels her destiny will be found in Normandy.

She keeps these thoughts to herself, resolving to honour her promise to Gudrun that she will have first refusal if she wants to give up the business. She decides that she will hand over to Gudrun without requiring any payment in recognition of the deep bond between them.

The new looms are installed, and Freya has trained her women in their use, although they are not much different from the old looms.

She frequently travels to the Saxon village to meet with Odella, with whom she is building a strong friendship. Most times she rides a horse lent to her by Dag. She also meets dressmakers to discuss styles, colours, and techniques. One of the benefits is that they all learn from each other. Odella has been spreading the word and she feels that responses from the Saxon women are positive. Odella has been meeting with women from other villages nearby on market days.

Freya concludes that, between the Viking and Saxon communities in a period of peace and cooperation, there is potential for a profitable business.

She offers a prayer to Frode through the Gods seeking his approval and support while reassuring him of her love and intention to be reunited with him. Yet again there is no identifiable answer.

While her parents are in Normandy, Freya arranges for the workshop to be fitted out, stocks of wool, silk, and dyes to be bought and stored. Dag has been fair in his negotiations on prices.

Freya, together with a couple of young local girls, daughters of one of Gudrun's many friends, prepare bales of wool for dyeing in red, yellow, green, blue, and black in a variety of shades. She has found a skilled fuller to manage the dyeing process. His brother is an experienced shearman. Freya is then freed to overview the whole business.

As matters develop she thinks it would be a good idea to invite Odella to be involved. She gets together with Odella to review progress and asks," would you be willing to supervise the dressmakers, particularly to ensure they work hard and maintain the high quality of work I require?"

"I would love to."

As the two women continue talking, Odella asks," may I make a suggestion?"

"Please do."

"I would like to offer my house for meeting customers and taking orders. It would save you much travelling and you could devote more time to getting business in Jorvic. We could meet frequently to review progress."

Freya, thinking hard, sees an opportunity, "why not? It makes sense. Let me talk to Gudrun and I will then speak with you further."

Freya meets with Gudrun the next to discuss employing Odella.

Gudrun, thoughtfully, says to Freya," as you know I was only intending to help you administer the business, particularly in finance. I am unable to give more, so I think you should offer Odella a share in the business, say twenty-five per cent. I would further suggest that you could hold sixty percent, with my holding the balance of fifteen percent. Freya considers the proposal quickly and realising the sense of it, agrees.

Two days later Freya calls on Odella and proposes," I have been talking to Gudrun as agreed and we would like to involve you directly in the business. We suggest you hold twenty-five percent, sharing in the profits after deduction of expenses. You and I would do the operational work, while Gudrun, holding fifteen percent, will look after administration and finance."

"I am thrilled to think you are trusting me and I accept gladly. However, I need Cedric's approval."

She calls out to Cedric, asking him to join them. Both explain the nature of the business and the role that Odella is being asked to play.

Cedric, never one to make hasty decisions nor unwilling to limit Odella's activities too much, asks many questions.

"Give me an hour or so to consider this. I may have more questions. I need to be sure that Odella can maintain her other duties."

Cedric wanders off while the women go for a walk round the settlement.

A little longer than expected, Cedric returns and asks more very searching questions, after which stands up and, embracing the two women, chuckles and says," I approve, but on condition that I review my consent in six months."

Jumping up and down with glee while Cedric leaves them, they go for another walk to discuss the way in which their arrangement will work. Odella readily agrees to all Freya's suggestions and they then work out the details.

On return to Jorvik Freya visits each weaver and spinner depositing the dyed wool with them for weaving into bolts of cloth. It takes several weeks for a supply of dyed wool to be assembled and checked for quality. Freya is very satisfied with the product.

Dag lends her a horse and cart by which she delivers the woven wool and quantities of yarn to the dressmakers in the Saxon village.

When delivering she speaks to each dressmaker giving them instructions, "please practice with some of this wool using any design of your choice. We will inspect your work and if we are satisfied we will confirm that you will work for me as agreed." She adds, "Odella has joined me in running the business and will be your supervisor."

During the next year, Freya, Odella and Gudrun slowly build up the business from the basis Freya has devised. Cedric has given his approval to Odella continuing. She quietly acknowledges to herself that without the help of the other two she could never have progressed as far.

After six months they feel that they have established a reputation for high quality work, imaginative designs using colour to great effect through a skilful and dedicated workforce.

One night Freya has a dream in which Frode appears. He seems to be saying," what you are doing is wonderful and I feel that the things you are learning will have a bearing on our future."

Freya caught up in the emotion of the dream replies, in the hope that Frode hears her, "Frode please stay with me or at least wait for me. I am coming. I don't know when, but I think it will be soon."

As the dream fades, Freya feels energised and is stimulated to work hard.

At that point Freya calls a meeting with Gudrun and Odella in Freya's workshop to review progress and discuss changes or innovations.

Freya, with some intensity, tells the others," we have been trading for a year with reasonable success. We are doing more business in Odella's village. Furthermore, we are getting orders from other nearby villages."

She continues, "we work well together, and I would like us to speak frankly about any changes we should make."

A lively discussion takes place during which Odella makes the point," we should stop trying to have a set of styles which do not reflect the attitudes of the two peoples. We should do designs specifically for each."

This change, along with a few others, is agreed upon.

Freya states, "while we are going to make these changes, let us not lose sight of the fact that our strength lies in high quality and prompt delivery. Our prices are high, but enough people are prepared to buy from us. I do not think that we should risk our reputation by growing too big.

After all, we are lucky enough not to rely on the business for a living! This is fun and enables us to do things we would not normally do."

The meeting breaks up, but Freya hangs back and ponders on how soon it must be before she moves on.

Meantime, her father is working hard with Dag and Hakon. He makes several visits to Normandy. During the next eighteen months Freya's business thrives within the limits she has agreed with her partners.

Then one day Gustav, after the family evening meal is over, announces, "Dag wants me to go to Normandy to set up a satellite trading business. We have discussed what he wants me to achieve, and I am certain I can, with your help."

Gustav continues," Dag will assemble a large supply of goods comprising furs, hides, wool, textiles and pottery."

He proceeds to outline in detail what the plans are.

"Freya, I know that you have a thriving business and accept that you may wish to stay in Jorvic, but I would like you to join me and use your experience to develop our business."

Freya, full of enthusiasm for a new challenge, readily agrees, "count me in!"

"Then it is agreed. Tomorrow we start planning the move to Normandy," replies Gustav.

That night Freya cannot sleep, for she is thinking that her reunion with Frode cannot be far away. She is concerned because she has no idea what form the reunion will take.

She prays to her Gods," please let Frode know that I am coming." As always there is no answer.

Gustav thinks that it will take some weeks to organise the move, settling his debts and other affairs. Transport will one of Dag's trading ships, as the move will be part of a normal trading run. As it is high summer they will not be prey to storms, although they are never ruled out.

Freya meets with Gudrun and Odella to tell them of what is to happen and, having previously agreed it with Gudrun, tells them that she will hand over the business to them without the need for payment, in recognition of the crucial part both have played in developing it.

Freya explains, "with each of you holding an equal share it might be difficult if you come into dispute. I have, therefore, arranged for an arbiter to rule on disputes. He is a senior councillor to the head of the Jorvic settlement, well versed in Viking law. He understands that Viking law will prevail over Saxon law in the event of conflict."

Freya continues, "this is a condition of your taking over. I am sure you will see the sense of this. In addition, Hakon will take over my parent's hut and will give you freedom of access to the workshop."

Both Gudrun and Odella agree and the handover goes smoothly to completion.

Three weeks later everything is settled; the longboat to Normandy loads up and sets sail. Freya is about to enter a new chapter in her life, which she faces with great excitement and some trepidation. Her mind is consumed with thoughts of meeting Frode again.

CHAPTER THIRTEEN

THE SEPARATION YEARS

FRODE IN KILKENNY IRELAND

As Frode strides out from Glendalough to the south he is filled with elation. Much as he enjoyed his sojourn at the monastery, he felt constrained and wanted to break out to enjoy freedom from rules and regulations. He is aware that to stay at Glendalough is not his destiny.

He has decided that he should strike out for the Viking settlement at Waterford. In the early evening of the first day out he stops off at a farm, offering to give the family there a few stories about Dyflin. In the discussion the farmer asks Frode, "you have the look of a Viking about you!"

Frode, admitting his ancestry, replies, "yes, but I spent a long up at Glendalough and converted to Christianity."

The farmer invites Frode into the house and offers him a meal, saying, "do join us in prayer and supper."

The family, in enjoying their meal, are finding Frode very well informed and amusing. The children are especially fascinated when Frode tells them of his childhood, the games he played with his friends and of the stories and acting.

Later in the evening the adults quiz him about Glendalough where he tells them of the experiences he had and of his conversion to Christianity.

The farmer, called Niall, wanting to know more of Viking folklore, asks, "tell us about the Nordic Gods, their names, and what they stood for."

Frode, casting his mind back, closes his eyes and starts to tell his tale of the Gods. He says that there is a hierarchy, that each God is responsible for at least one thing. "I give you the example of Freya, the Goddess of love and fertility. Her task is to ensure that the Viking race grows and in so doing, she oversees the meeting of Viking men and women and encourages them to fall in love and have families."

The farmer's wife, Clodagh, is very interested in Frode as a person and wants to know more of his background.

Frode explains, "When I was a child I was part of a group of children which took part in plays to entertain people in our settlement. The lead was a beautiful, charismatic girl called Freya who had great skill in helping children to act in plays. She and I worked very closely together in the production of these plays.

Clodagh interjects, "were you in love with her?"

"Yes. There is a prophesy that we will create a dynasty which will achieve enormous influence and power. We do not know how or when this is going to happen. All I know is that I love her deeply. Like most of my friends I was driven to leave Nordland and seek adventure and my fortune elsewhere. It is normal in Viking society. This is why I am in Ireland"

Frode continues," you may have heard there was a big battle outside Dyflyn in which the Vikings were defeated. The Abbot at Glendalough suggested that, for my own safety, I should move on. I am on my way to Waterford to see if I can settle for a little while"

Clodagh, sensing that Frode is ready to talk and weave a heartfelt true story, asks, "do you know anything of what has happened Freya?"

"No, although I am a Christian and pray to God, I also pray to the Nordic Gods, asking them all to keep Freya safe. I have had no response from any of them. As a Christian, however, I have faith that she is well and prospering."

For the first time in a long time Frode, in telling this story from his heart, finds himself at peace. He is absorbed by Clodagh's gentleness and perception. He relaxes in Clodagh's presence.

He talks of his time in Glendalough, his conversion and the fellowship with the brothers there. He talks of his confusion about wanting to settle in the safety and comfort of Glendalough yet having a need to move on.

What he does not know is that Clodagh comes from a background of Irish mystics who had a deep knowledge of the human condition, transcending anything ascribed to Christian theology. With this skill she is able join her mind with Frode's and bring him peace and tranquillity which will sustain him in his travels.

At the end of the evening Niall offers Frode prayers to safeguard Freya which Frode accepts. He then retires to sleep. His sense of wellbeing is heightened by the warmth of the fellowship he has experienced. During the night he is aware of Freya being nearer to him than Nordland and watching over him, through which he is convinced that she is fit and well.

After a full night's sleep Frode joins the family for breakfast. Clodagh packs a supply of food in his knapsack. As he takes his leave he thanks them for their hospitality and asks that he would like to offer a little advice to Niall and Clodagh's young sons. The parents agree so Frode calls the boys to him, saying, " come, walk with me a little way down the road as I would like to talk to you."

It is raining as they walk along the edge of a field leading to the track which will take Frode towards Waterford he says to the children,

"You live in a beautiful country with a history of which you should be proud. As you grow older you will realise that you have both inherited a perceptive nature. Listen to it and obey it. Always do what is right and follow your destiny as it is revealed to you. I am following mine now as I leave you. Your mother is the most perceptive person I have ever known. Fare thee well and thank you for your company."

The children both realise that Frode is serious and they agree that they must take Frode's advice," we will, we will," they exclaim as they hop skip and jump for joy on the way back home.

With that Frode strides ahead towards Waterford, turns once to wave goodbye and thinks, "yes, I am following my destiny through this green and wonderful land, but I cannot linger too long."

CHAPTER FOURTEEN

THE SEPARATION YEARS

FRODE IN WATERFORD (VEORAFJOROR)

As Frode walks purposefully south to Waterford the rain clouds part, permitting a weak watery sun to break through. He never ceases to marvel at the soft green beauty of the land. "There is no harshness here. There is no war or pillaging. This is a blessed and pleasant land. "Maybe our God of peace, Baldur, has influence here," he thinks.

He thinks he can reach Waterford in two days, but he has hardly formed the thought when he sees a group of grubby little urchins playing in the mud at the side of a slow-moving stream. On seeing him the children run away. Frode decides to sit by the stream to rest a while. Not long afterwards he notices the children are slowly returning as their curiosity gets the better of them. A girl of about 10 years of age is braver than the others and creeps closer. Frode quietly looks towards the girl saying, "my name is Frode. What's your name?" Hesitantly the girl, looking round to her friends who are still shyly hanging back, announces with more confidence, "Shelagh. Who are you and what are you doing?"

Frode replies," I am a travelling storyteller on my way to Waterford and I have decided to rest by this beautiful stream for a little while."

Shelagh is now much more confident and at ease, "so you are a storyteller, are you? We have storytellers come to our farms. Would you tell us a story now?"

"Of course, I would love to do that"

Shelagh jumps up and calls to her friends," this man is a storyteller and I have asked him to tell us a story. Come on, this will be fun"

The children abandon their fears, as they trust Shelagh as their leader, and gather round in a semi- circle. Grubby they may be, but they are bright- eyed and eager to listen.

Frode decides to tell them of Nordland and the scenery which is so different from that in Ireland. He starts off,

"I am a Viking and come from a land far to the north which has huge mountains covered in snow and ice with steep sides leading to deep fjords."

Shelagh looks quizzical and interrupts, "what's a fjord?"

Frode, stopping to gather his thoughts on how to explain something outside the children's experience, draws a picture in the mud which fascinates the children while gaining their understanding quickly. He continues his tale, describing in wonderous detail the nature of his homeland. The children constantly interrupt, and he frequently explains by sketching in the mud.

Frode revels in his skill being displayed to an appreciative audience, especially children.

Eventually Shelagh says, "we must go home now. Thank you for being so kind. I would like to visit your country someday."

"Come on gang, we must go now and let our friend go on his way."

The children stand up, jump across the stream, turn, and wave farewell before skipping happily across the field.

Frode remains sitting for a little while, overwhelmed by the desire to have children of his own with Freya. He is deeply conscious at this moment that the prophesy will, and must, come true.

He has a meal from the food given to him by Clodagh, gets up, stretches, offers a prayer of thanks to God for his being given the pleasure of the children's company and then he moves on.

Towards the end of the day Frode is aware that he is still a fair way from Waterford and thinks about finding some shelter for the night. As the light is fading he is aware of a great weariness coming over him. On seeing a small farmhouse, he approaches, ignoring the barking dog which seems to be "all noise and no action." He knocks on the door and waits. The dog, growling, is keeping its distance. Eventually the door is opened a little by a small child who peers at him through wide open deep blue eyes. The child makes no other move until Frode asks, "are your mummy and daddy at home?"

The child, saying nothing, scuttles back inside the house after slamming the door shut. Eventually a very large man comes to the door asking in an aggressive voice, "who are you and what do you want?"

Frode replies," I am a travelling storyteller and I was wondering if I could sleep in your barn tonight. I promise I will give you no trouble"

"Well, you may but I don't want you near the house and I expect you to be gone at first light tomorrow."

"Thank you for agreeing."

Frode then wanders over to the barn, pretending not to notice the little girl peering through a window.

The dog ambles into the barn, pauses to lick Frode's hand and then settles down beside Frode to be stroked.

Frode makes himself comfortable, and after eating the last of his food, falls into a deep sleep. He dreams of Freya, remembering times they enjoyed together. He is aware the bond between them is strengthening despite their not having seem each other for a long time.

Suddenly he becomes aware of Freya's spirit presence in the barn. She is saying," I miss you my love, but I know that we will meet very soon. Please continue onwards with determination."

Frode sits up and shouts out, "I will, I promise!"

He then lies back and falls asleep again, feeling a great surge of energy flowing through him.

Next morning, at first light, as he prepares to leave, he sees the little girl at the door. She is timidly holding a jug of milk, some bread and goat's cheese. After laying them on the ground she skips back to the house where her mother is standing by the door.

Frode eats his breakfast after which he takes his leave, but not before waving his thanks to the little girl and her mother. The dog follows for a while until he is called back by the girl.

Frode is still amazed at the hospitality he is being shown by the Irish people.

Once again dark clouds are gathering with rain squalls showing in the distance. By now Frode is well used to the unpredictable weather but he wishes, sometimes, that the rain was less heavy and frequent. The cloak that Ronan gave him does not always give full protection.

With his head down, he walks purposefully into the rain which is coming down in torrents, he intends to reach Waterford well before nightfall.

In the late afternoon the rain clears, the sun shines out causing rain drops on tree branches to sparkle. Myriad birds add their songs to the uplifting scene, while wild flowers are showing in their colourful glory all of which do much to raise Frode's miserable and damp spirits.

"I am almost regretting setting out on this venture. It is only the thought of meeting my beloved Freya again that makes it bearable," he mutters to himself.

Then the calmness that Clodagh had placed in his sub conscious mind washes over him and he has a feeling of guilt.

Raising his head high he continues for a little while until he sees smoke on the horizon indicating the closeness of Waterford.

As he gets nearer he passes several small and well- tended farms where he exchanges friendly greetings with people on them. He is impressed by the way the farms are kept in good repair. Here he thinks, "there has been peace here for some time"

As he gets nearer the main settlement he realises that it is not large, counting thirty huts and one longhouse. There are the usual businesses such as blacksmiths, workshops' and grain stores. He even thinks he sees a storyteller and wryly thinks he would find swapping stories would be fun.

As he strides towards the longhouse he is assailed by smells he has not experienced since Dyflyn and they are more noticeable after his having spent so much time in the clean air of the countryside.

He exchanges greetings with many of the people and is surrounded by children looking at him with curiosity.

He stops by a man who seems to be the settlement's storyteller asking," where do I find the chief ?"

Pointing towards the longhouse the man enquires, "where are you from then?"

"I am from Nordland via Dyflyn and the Glendalough Monastery," comes the reply from Frode, with a huge grin on his face.

"Well now, my name is Peter, comes the rejoinder, maybe we can meet later to exchange news. If you have nowhere to stay, please call on me. I live in the hut just across the way."

"I would love to stay with you and swap stories. Until later then," says Frode as he carries on to the longhouse.

On reaching the longhouse the children all scamper off, attracted by a couple of dogs tussling over a large bone. A small man ambles round from the side of the building, "can I help you he asks? -I am Cathal, the leader of the community. I live alone here following the death of my wife some years ago."

Frode in explaining who he is, adds, "I'd like to stay in the settlement for a while"

"Come into the house and we'll talk. We always welcome visitors of Viking stock and the opportunity to hear of what is happening outside our settlement."

They go inside and talk for a long time, exchanging news and views, with Frode speaking of his varied farming background.

Later in the night Cathal offers Frode his hospitality with a meal and a sleeping area which Frode gratefully accepts.

The following morning, after a light breakfast, Frode and Cathal discuss what Frode might want to do in Waterford and how long he might stay. Frode indicates, "I have a mission and will need to move on but, I would like to spend some time here. I met your settlement storyteller,

Peter as I arrived yesterday, and he would like to spend time with me exchanging stories. This would enrich our stock of stories. He also offered me accommodation, if I wanted it. Would you mind if I accepted? I do not wish to be ungrateful."

"Of course not. I do, however, have a suggestion to make in view of your farming background. There is a lady, newly widowed, with two teenage children, trying to manage her farm. She could do with some help for a while to run the farm and learn from an expcrienced person with farming background. Would you consider helping? Please think about it as you settle in with Peter."

Frode, with some uncertainty, "of course I will consider it. I will come back to you as soon as I can."

Cathal is happy with that and says," I will introduce you to Marla and the boys when you are ready. I really would appreciate your help. You see, Marla was a close friend of my late wife."

Frode takes his leave and goes wandering around, absorbing the friendly atmosphere and observing how busy everybody is. It is market day and the whole settlement is active in buying and selling with vendors calling out their wares. Farmers and artisans travel in from the surrounding area. The scenes are reminiscent of the busy carnivals he watched in Dyflin.

As he stops to chat to a group of musicians, preparing to set up a singing session using harps, he sees Peter waving to him. As he promises to return to hear the singers he goes to meet Peter. Peter is curious, "what did you do last night?"

"I spent a long time chatting to Cathal who seems very lonely following his wife's death."

Peter agrees, "yes, Cathal spends lots of time with me and my family. He is welcome, and we enjoy his company."

"So," says Peter, "what would you like to do, sit and talk?"

Frode agrees and they go to the edge of the settlement, but pause, listening for a while to the musicians playing lively, happy music. The audience is large, and everybody joins in in the singing and dancing.

Suddenly Frode finds himself caught up in the dancing with a girl in a light- coloured swirling dress. She has long red hair flowing freely as the music captures the magic of the scene. Frode glances towards Peter trying to say "sorry" but Peter merely smiles and waits. When the dance is over and the girl flounces away, smiling, to join her friends on the fringe of the crowd, Frode goes back to Peter, apologising for his bad manners. Peter says," do not worry. You were privileged to be selected by the most desirable girl in the area. Beware, though, she is likely to tease you out of your mind!" Frode ponders for a moment and reminds himself of his covenant with Freya.

"Come, let's go talk, shall we?" Peter is happy to agree as, like all storytellers, he is excited by the prospect of hearing new stories and tales of adventure. Frode starts by telling of his childhood in Nordland, particularly of the plays he was involved in. He tells of Freya and the prophesy. Peter frequently interrupts with questions.

"Please describe Freya and tell me more of the prophesy and how you now regard it. Do you still believe it will come true?"

"Yes, I do believe it to be true and that I am following the path to the reunion with Freya. I believe that our Nordic Gods are preparing both of us to achieve our destiny."

Frode then goes on to describe Freya in detail.

"You seem to have found a most wondrous lady worthy of your devotion and I am sure that you will be reunited," comments Peter.

"How long do you intend to stay here, and where are you going after that?"

"I really don't know. I am a wanderer now being drawn to a place where I meet Freya again. However, I would like to live in, and explore, this settlement for a while."

Peter ponders for a moment, then comments," please stay for as long as you can as I am sure we can have a wonderful time working together."

"I shall, but I will need to find work."

CHAPTER FIFTEEN

THE SEPARATION YEARS

FRODE CONTINUES IN WATERFORD

Frode, sometimes accompanied by Peter, spends several days exploring the settlement. Peter is a jeweller of great renown in the area and he proudly shows Frode round his workshops.

"As you will see," says Peter, noticing Frode's awestruck expression, we work in gold, silver, amber, and different coloured stones. I have a team of twenty all of whom are experienced smiths. Our best-selling items are amber mounted in silver brooches." Peter goes to fetch a piece of beautiful craftsmanship to show Frode. Frode sees a brooch formed of a complex runic design made of silver with amber insets. It is quite the most exquisite piece of jewellery he has ever seen. In his mind's eye he sees the brooch as a gift to Freya and asks Peter if he can buy it. Peter agrees, and a price is offered which Frode pays. He then stores it safely in a pouch hidden strapped to his back.

After a few days when the two of them sit in the marketplace telling stories, to children, Peter suggests he takes Frode for a tour of the harbour.

As is to be expected in a Viking port, the scene is one of hustle and bustle. They wander around while Peter introduces Frode to some merchants and sea captains. As it is not long before Frode is gossiping with all and sundry, Peter leaves him to it and returns to his workshop, with a promise to meet him again in the evening.

One captain regularly sails to Normandy. He tells Frode of the strong successful settlements, particularly of those in Normandy, where Caen and Rouen are communities in trading and the manufacture of clothing and jewellery. Frode begins to wonder what this might mean to him as he is beginning to feel that he must surely meet Freya soon and wants to learn more. However, he is distracted by a merchant selling spices and other goods he has never seen before. He goes over to talk to the merchant who explains that much of his merchandise comes from countries far to the east. Frode is entranced by the merchant's stories of Viking adventures and the creation of large trading groups. Frode vows to return to meet and talk with the merchant with the idea that he can add new features to his stories.

He is inspired by what he has seen and heard and returns to meet Peter. Over a meal, comprising bread and fish, he tells Peter of his experience. Peter, who's jewellery market is largely local begins to think about expansion. He wonders if he can export his goods to other Viking settlements outside Ireland and sees the possibility of Frode becoming his agent, or even partner. They discuss the idea at length, but Frode is aware that as he has no understanding the business and is not entirely sure he wants that kind of involvement.

Peter indicates," I am happy to train you, both in design and jewellery making. It will take time, but I am sure that you will become good enough"

Frode, realising that this is an opportunity not to be missed, "I accept that this would be an experience worth acquiring."

The following morning Frode visits Cathal to explain to him why he will be unable to help Marga. He is unwilling to say that he does not want to be tied down and restricts his explanation to an outline of his long-term plan to move on to follow his destiny.

Cathal, disappointed, says," I think I understand and, of course, accept your response. Please always feel free to call on me while you are here, as you will be welcome."

As he goes along the breakwater back towards Peter's workshop, he is mobbed by excited children demanding he tell them a story.

Against a background of noise from the sailors' activities on their boats and the squealing of sea gulls constantly scavenging, Frode says, "Gather round then and I will tell you one."

Peter appears, claiming, "what's all this about then?" The children answer, "Frode is going to tell us a story."

Peter, smiling, "can I join in?"

The children are happy and Frode opens with a question.

"Children, do you know what it's like to make a long sea journey in a longboat?"

There is a chorus of, "no, tell us, please"

Peter chips in, "I can make howling wind noises and sing the songs of the sailors as Frode goes along."

Frode, looking at Peter, raises a quizzical eyebrow, "what do you know about that?"

"You wait until I tell stories of my visit to Novgorod. You will be amazed!"

"Where's Novgorod?" "Ah ha, wait and see!"

To an enraptured audience growing, quickly as children and adults wander in, Frode and Peter work together with word and sound effects producing a story of a long and hazardous journey to Normandy in a cargo longboat. The longboat arrives safely which Frode claims is thanks to the care of Nordic Gods. The children are puzzled by the reference to Nordic Gods. Before Frode can explain, an adult, standing at the fringe exclaims, "that cannot be. There is only one true God!"

Thinking quickly, Frode replies," I was telling of a time prior to Vikings being converted to Christianity. Before I came here I studied at the monastery at Glendalough where I became a Christian."

Only a little mollified, the adult asked, "why then do you not tell Bible stories."

"I can and do when asked. However, a good storyteller should cover as many topics as he can in order that he can entertain a wide range of people."

Nothing more is said and the crowd drifts away as Frode promises to tell some Bible stories in the future.

To Peter he says," It would be good if we came to this spot amid all the hustle and bustle of the harbour. Let's try it and see"

"Well worth a try," replies Peter.

The next day Frode begins his apprenticeship in jewellery making under Peter's supervision. Later on, he will work with the other smiths.

"Why not try to produce some initial designs yourself," suggests Peter.

Frode, willing to try something new, agrees, lamenting, "I am no artist!"

"Do not worry. I, or one of the experienced designers, will help you interpret ideas. All you have to do is produce an outline of your idea. If it's good, we will turn it into a piece of jewellery."

For over a year Frode divides his time learning to design and manufacture jewellery, storytelling by the harbour and meeting longboat crew who vie with one another to add details of their experiences for him to create more stories. In his promise earlier he includes Bible stories in his repertoire.

He and Peter, working together, bring hours of interest and amusement to children who flock to them every day. Adults often stop by to listen, including the adult who wanted them to tell Bible stories.

One day they become aware of a boy and a girl around eight years of age being constantly in the audience and who listen intently to the stories.

Frode wonders why and asks them to join him when the story session is finished.

Frode asks them," why do you watch us so closely?"

The boy hanging his head down mutters shyly," I would like to tell stories like you do."

"Me too," exclaims the little girl, with an engaging smile and who is much more confident.

Frode casts his mind back to his boyhood in Narvik and the joy he experienced during that time when he told stories to his friends and worked so closely with his beloved Freya.

He ponders for a moment, then smiling broadly, asks the children," what are your names?"

"Connel and Kathleen," they chorus.

" Well now, what do you remember of the story I told you about the little people in the wood near Glendalough?"

Connel and Kathleen vie with one another to repeat large parts of the story, much to Frode and Peter's pleasure.

Frode to think about how to use their enthusiasm in such a way that they enjoy what they do and share that joy with others.

Frode and Peter discuss their thoughts and conclude that the best way is to have the children sit with them during the story telling and interject comments. To begin with Frode will prepare the comments for them to say so that they learn and gain confidence.

Next morning, after the audience has left, Peter returns to his workshop, and Frode sits down with Connel and Kathleen.

"I have an idea. How would you both like to take part in the storytelling? You could take over part of the story. Peter and I will train you. Then, if you are good enough and want to, you could make up your own stories and tell them alongside ours. We would make a fantastic team!"

Both children reply in great excitement, "yes please."

Each morning, before the audience gathers, Frode and Peter take Connel and Kathleen through their roles. He soon realises that both children have talent and learn quickly. Their parents come with them and are impressed by their performance. They go to Frode saying to him,"this is wonderful work that you are doing. The children are so enthusiastic and enjoy it so much."

Frode replies," they are so talented that I hope to be able to encourage them to tell stories to their own audiences. That would give me the greatest pleasure."

While the storytelling develops into a popular activity in the community, with people flocking to the harbour to hear the stories, Frode continues to learn jewellery design and manufacture. He finds this totally absorbing and is proving to have the talent and the skills to produce work that Peter believes will sell. After a few months Frode is selling pieces successfully.

In between all this activity he meets ship captains and crew members, hearing their tales of their experiences, adding them to his store of stories. Connel and Kathleen join him and are enthralled by what they hear. The sailors appreciate the children's interest.

However, during this time, Frode is becoming unsettled and feels the urge to move on. One day I know I must settle, but only with my beloved Freya. The storytelling is developing as hoped and soon the children have their own audiences. Frode feels he is going to get bored and needs a change. He wonders if it's because he is thinking of Freya constantly.

One evening, after a sailor had regaled him with tales of Normandy and of Caen in particular, he has a dream. He is in a place he does not recognise, sketching jewellery designs when Freya appears next to him. She whispers in his ear, "I need you. I am in Normandy with my parents. Wherever you are, leave, and come to me. The Gods are telling me the time has come for the prophesy to come true."

Frode tries to reply, but, frustratingly, the vision fades quickly.

Unbeknown to them, the Nordic Gods, in a special convocation have decided that Frode and Freya are ready for their reunion.

Next day Frode decides to take stock of his situation and asks Peter to hear him and give him advice.

They are taking a break and are sitting in the sun, outside the workshop.

"Peter," he says," I would like your help in my trying to work out just where I am. I am getting strong feelings that Freya and I will meet again very soon, and I want to feel that I am ready."

Peter responds, "I am happy to listen and comment as necessary."

Frode takes a deep breath and gives an outline of his thoughts.

"I am an experienced storyteller and working with you has been a joy. We have, I hope, set a tradition in story telling here in Waterford where children are key players.

I have learned about jewellery design and manufacture and, thanks to your patience I think, will be able to be useful to a manufacturer."

Peter interjects, "there is no doubt you have acquired all the basic skills, particularly in design. You have a natural talent."

"Thank you, Peter. I also have farming skills and through my time at Glendalough I have learned patience, a little humility and a knowledge of how to manage people."

Peter, chortling loudly, "humility, don't make me laugh my friend, but then you must always stand your ground!"

Both then become silent for a while, while they think. Eventually, Peter breaks the silence.

"I am sad at the thought of losing your company. It has been a great adventure. However, you did speak of your destiny when we first met, and I do believe you are right to think that the time has come to move on."

"What are your thoughts, Frode?"

"Firstly, please accept my thanks for your support and honesty. I now must think some more and see where I must go and how I can get there. Fortunately, I do not have much in the way of possessions and I have saved a fair amount of silver."

Peter goes back into the workshop, leaving Frode to think.

A little while later Peter re-joins Frode, saying, "I would like you to have some of the jewellery pieces you designed and helped to make. You could show these pieces to a prospective employer. They are exceptionally good."

Frode is overwhelmed, exclaiming "you are so generous. Thank you. I am delighted to accept."

Peter stands up, "come on then, let's stop chattering and get some serious work done before you leave. We have a few weeks left and there some special techniques I must teach you!"

In between further storytelling mornings at the harbour, Frode spends time seeking the captain he had met who goes to Normandy regularly.

Three weeks later the longboat from Normandy arrives. Frode waits until after the cargo is discharged and then sees the captain call into a nearby tavern.

Frode approaches the captain," do you remember me? My name is Frode. We spoke when I came to Waterford two years ago."

The captain stands up, saying," yes, I do remember you. You are the storyteller are you not? My children chatter all the time about your stories. My name is Jarl. What can I do for you?"

"I want to go to Normandy. Could I sail with you on your next journey? "

"Of course," replies Jarl. "I cannot take passengers, so you would have to work your passage. You are a strong looking man, so you would be a valuable crew member. Would you be willing?"

This suits Frode well as it enables him to save his cash."I accept," says Frode.

Jarl extends his hand to shake, exclaiming," It's a deal. I don't know when we next sail-it all depends on what cargo is on offer. Call by each day to check with me."

Frode is so full of excitement that for some time he fails to notice a gaggle of children trailing along behind him as he returns to Peter's workshop. When he does so, he stops, gathers the children round him and makes up a story as he goes along about a storyteller who must make a long journey to meet a lady he has not seen for years and who he loves very much.

As the story unfolds, little Kathleen jumps up and down exclaiming, "it's you, it's you isn't it?

Frode stops and says, "yes, it is. I must go, but I will miss you all very much. Kathleen and Connel should carry on telling stories if you wish. There follows a loud chorus of, "please do not go!"

"I really have to, but I know Kathleen and Connel will carry on the tradition I hope I have set up. Remember, too, that Peter will still be here, as he was long before I came."

The children are sad and quiet as Frode finishes his story. The children follow him back to Peter's workshop before going off to play on the beach near the harbour.

Back at the workshop Frode waits for Peter to finish a piece of jewellery and then says, "I have found a captain willing to take me to Normandy.

All I have to do is wait until he has enough cargo to take. I have told the children."

Peter, replies," that's fine. You will have a few days to prepare. I need you to select the jewellery pieces. May I suggest we continue to tell stories at the harbour until you go."

Every day for nearly two weeks Frode calls on Jarl after story telling. Jarl is concerned, as autumn is approaching with its attendant storms, that the boat must sail within the next week even if it is not full. Fortunately, he has enough cargo booked already to make the sailing viable.

Jarl, concerned Frode will be a stranger in Normandy, calls him over to a quiet area on the quay, saying, "I am concerned that you do not know anybody in Normandy. I have a friend in Caen who makes and sells pottery. I would be happy to introduce you to him. I am sure he would have you stay at his house, with his family, until you find your feet."

Frode, exclaims with delight, "to be frank I was just a little worried about what would happen with my arriving in a strange place without contacts. Thank you so much for being so kind."

"That's settled then," says Jarl, clapping Frode on the shoulder.

Meanwhile Frode visits Cathal to make his farewells. He learns that Marla is coping well with assistance from the father of one of her son's friends. Cathal thinks they might marry.

Then one bright, but windy morning Frode meets with Jarl who tells him they are to sail early the following day. Frode hurries back to Peter's workshop to pack up his few belongings.

The next day Peter announces," I will come with you to the harbour."

The wind of the previous day, which has been worrying Frode has abated. When he reaches the longship, Jarl shows him where to stow his gear and informs Frode that he will be an oarsman, as he does not have the skill to set and take down sails or use the steering oar.

Frode shrugs his shoulders. "So be it. I will pull my weight."

Jarl, laughing loudly, "do you realise what you have just said?"

Frode, not a little embarrassed, but laughing too, "sorry!"

Jarl is satisfied and shows Frode his place on the rowing bench, introducing him to the other rowing crew.

"the crew will show you what to do. There is a skill to rowing, but, provided you do exactly what you are told, you will manage well. You look strong enough!"

Once he has settled, Frode returns to the quayside to the sound of cheering. He is overwhelmed to see a huge crowd of children and adults waiting there. He is so moved that he climbs down to the quay and goes through the people shaking hands and exchanging good wishes.

When he has done that, and with Jarl's permission he and Peter climb up onto the prow of the longship. Peter calls for attention. When the cheering and talking has died down, Frode addresses the crowd.

"I am touched by your caring and love. I am privileged to have lived among you and shared so many experiences. I thank my friend Peter here for teaching me jewellery making skills and for sharing the story telling. I commend Connel and Kathleen. They have wonderful talent and will work with Peter to continue the tradition."

Connel and Kathleen are at the front of the crowd and suddenly two burly sailors hand the children up to stand next to Frode and Peter. With hugs and tears the four make their very personal farewells, to the cheering and hand clapping from the crowd.

Jarl moves near to Frode and says, "we must sail now."

The children and Peter return to the quay as the crowds watch the crew preparing to leave.

Jarl, as a concession to the occasion, allows Frode to stay at the prow waving his farewell until the ship has moved well down channel to the open sea.

Frode then takes his place at the rowing bench with Jarl's comment in his ears, "you'll have to work hard now, lad!"

Unseen by Frode, Cathal and Marla are watching from the headland overlooking the harbour.

CHAPTER SIXTEEN

THE SEPARATION YEARS

FREYA AND FAMILY SETTLE IN NORMANDY

Freya's parents are well aware of the risks they are taking in sailing so late in the season. Freya has taken great care to pack her precious dresses in waterproof material as she will need these as samples if she wishes to establish her business in Normandy. Even if she does not, she will present a figure of elegance as often as she can and local fashion permits.

The journey takes six days in weather conditions, while making the sea quite rough, are quite benign for the time of year.

The ship calls in at an old Roman fort, now a small Viking settlement, to be known in later times as Reculver, in the south of England, to top up provisions and make some repairs to the sail.

Freya takes the chance to meet local women to gossip.

After spending a couple of days there, the ship sets off again, carrying a young couple, Halvar and Eira (originally Danish Vikings) who want to settle in Normandy. They become friends of Freya and for the rest of the voyage they are inseparable.

They talk about the societies in which they grew up, being interested in the differences between the cultures.

The voyage is uneventful, and the ship is rowed upriver from the Normandy coast to dock in Caen. The port is all hustle and bustle with goods being moved about, people, some just loafing about while awaiting opportunities for work, others intently following their business. Amidst all this activity Freya's parents seek help in unloading their goods. It turns out that there are plenty of helpers there. Freya organises the labour force while Ranveya finds a man with a horse and cart for hire. Gustav wanders off to find temporary accommodation.

He has no problem finding temporary warehousing for his trade goods and returns to the ship immediately to arrange the unloading and transport to the warehouse.

Halvar and Eira gather their few belongings, make their farewells and stride off having admitted that they have no idea where they are going and what they are going to do.

Just before they go, Freya whispers in Eira's ear," stay here. This is where we are going to establish a trading business linked to the one in Jorvic I told you about."

Eira, with a grin, replies, "are you plotting something? I think you are. Let's see, shall we? Meantime it's been wonderful to meet you and your family. Farewell."

Gustav returns, claiming," I found decent accommodation which will suit us for a week or so while we gather all the things we need to set up permanently.

Freya says," Can I come with you when you go to buy all these things? I'd like to watch you bargaining!"

"Why not. It will be fun. We'll go tomorrow and see what's available. I just hope the local dealers take us for fools, eh?"

"Just let me at 'em," chuckles Freya.

The family get together after an evening meal to plan a course of action.

Ranveya, in a determined tone of voice, states," the first thing we must do is find a place to live. If necessary, we build one. I would prefer that as we can have a layout that suits us."

Gustav and Freya, knowing better than to argue, agree, "why don't you search for the house or land upon which to build while we search for a permanent warehouse."

All agree on that course of action.

Ranveya quickly realises that there is no way that she can avoid their designing and building their own house. She explains her reasoning to Gustav and Freya. Beforehand she has spoken to people who will build the house for them and obtained an estimate of the cost. There is plenty of timber and thatch available and the estimated cost is reasonable. The idea is agreed, and they sit down to sketch out a design following the traditional longhouse design. They agree that Ranveya meets the builders, who also offer a piece of land free of cost, the next day.

Gustav, however, is disappointed that he has not yet found a suitable property for his warehouse. Until this is done he cannot open negotiations to form the trading links he needs if he is to honour his business agreement with Dag in Jorvic.

Freya is having doubts about trying to establish a dress making business as she feels that it is a great deal of hard work for very little return. She is now more interested in the trading business and feels she can contribute to it.

After their morning meal and before Gustav goes out to continue his search for a warehouse, Freya says," I have been thinking and believe I would prefer to work with you, father, in the business. I believe I have acquired real experience through my business in Jorvic. "What do you think?"

Gustav, who is in the process of pulling on his boots and breathing heavily from the effort, snorts,"I never thought you were ever going to ask!"

Looking at Ranveya for support which she gives with a slight nod of her head, Gustav continues, "I would like nothing better. Well done! Come on, let's do it and find us a warehouse.

Freya smiles happily asking, "will you give me a few minutes to change my dress?"

After what appears to be an age, Freya returns to the room wearing an outstanding full length brown woollen dress which she created in Jorvic, into which she has added a blend of reds and greens.

Gustav and Ranveya are speechless at first, for they have never seen the dress before.

Freya, however, wonders," is it too rich and stylish for a trader's daughter?"

"On the contrary, it shows that you have created wealth from successful trading. People will look up to you and want to trade with you," says Ranveya.

Gustav says to Freya, "I think we should check over our stock to ensure it is all there and in good condition. Also, we'll be able to gauge the size of warehouse or trading space we need."

While Ranveya goes to meet builders, Gustav and Freya walk down to the docks. On the way they are frequently greeted by people they pass, and they stop to chat from time to time. They explain that they are newly arrived from Jorvic and are intending to set up a trading business as an extension one in Jorvic.

They quickly learn that Caen is less of a bullion economy, relying more on silver, and silver coin. While their wealth comprises much silver, they realise that a significant amount is in bullion. However, they hear that there are number of silversmiths nearby willing to buy bullion for coin. The trick is to negotiate hard-something that does not give Gustav or Freya much concern.

As they approach the docks, they pass a couple of men standing talking outside a warehouse.Gustav approaches them and asks," do you know of any available warehouse space we could buy or rent, we are looking for a size of around one "Mal"?"

One of them replies, "if you go down the side of the dock on your right and ask for Karl someone will find him and bring him to you. If anybody knows he will. Beware, though, he's drives very hard bargains."

They thank the men and walk down the dock as directed.

As always, the scene is one of apparent chaos, but as Freya stops to look, she realises that there is order and an atmosphere of purpose. A group of men are watching a longboat being moored and Gustav approaches them, "do any of you know Karl?"

"Oh yes," replies one. "if you go to that green painted building you will find him."

In thanking the man, they stroll over to the building. The doors are open, and they step in calling, "is Karl there?"

A well-dressed man comes forward from behind a stack of bales of cloth, "that's me. Can I help you?"

He cannot take his eyes off Freya as her appearance is at its elegant best. Freya, of course, pretends not to notice while Gustav get straight to the point.

"I am called Gustav, and this is my daughter, Freya. We have come from Jorvic to set up a trading company linked to one there. We are told you are the man to talk to about our acquiring some warehouse space near here."

"I may be able to help you. How much space do you need?"

"About twenty-five Rode, I think"

Meantime Freya is looking around and concludes that the location is excellent, and that Karl is well established.

Karl says, "I have nothing available at the moment."

"However, if you come with me, I will introduce to a friend who should be able to help as he has a warehouse in the next street which he does not fully use."

Karl yells, "Astrid, I am going out for a while."

With a smile Karl says, "Astrid is my wife and business partner."

The three of them walk down the street. Heavy rain the night before has helped wash away much of the dirt and rubbish, but Freya must raise her skirts to prevent soiling. As they reach Karl's friend's building a large dog appears. He approaches aggressively, but Freya offers her hand to the dog which stops being aggressive and licks it gently. Karl, with a look of disbelief on his face, exclaims,

"that dog is supposed to be the fiercest in the docks! Freya you must have a way with animals."

Freya just smiles as she continues to stroke the dog.

On reaching the massive warehouse Karl leads the way in and calls for Olag who appears silently by their side which make Freya jump.

When embracing Karl, Olag apologises for frightening Freya who smiles sweetly saying," apology accepted!"

Karl speaks to Olag, "These people are Gustav and Freya and they are looking to acquire about twenty-five Rode of storage and trading space. I told them you might be able to help."

Olag, stroking his chin and eyeing up Freya, "come with me."

They go out to the side of the building to a section at the rear. It is in excellent condition. There are stairs up to a first floor. There is a separate entrance and the road access is wide and free of obstructions.

Olag opens the large double doors to a large open area. It is self-contained and clear of rubbish, being a little larger than Gustav feels he requires, but otherwise ideal. Gustav and Freya are left to check the whole area out. After a thorough survey Freya says to Gustav, "This is ideal don't you agree? We need two employees anyway and they can live on the first floor and be security guards.

Gustav is happy to agree. He just wishes that he had found it when he was searching.

Gustav calls over to Karl to join them, while Olag goes back to his own warehouse.

"We would like to acquire this space as it suits us well. We will go to see Olag to see if we can do a deal. We would like to pay you a fee."

Karl replies, "I know I have a reputation for being a hard bargainer, but I do not think it right to accept a fee. However, I would like to collaborate with you as I think we would all gain from it.

Gustav shakes Karl's hand, "agreed."

Gustav and Freya go back to see Olag and discuss terms for leasing the warehouse space and get permission for employees to live there, with their acting as guards too. They know it has been unused for some time, but, bearing in mind they are new to Caen, and need to build up a reputation of fair dealing they think it best to haggle just a little as haggling is expected. Olag, however, quotes a figure which is outrageously high. Freya cannot contain herself while Gustav's face is impassive.

Freya, getting a "go ahead signal from Gustav," starts laughing and says" that's outrageous." She counters with an offer of less than fifty percent.

It's Olag's turn to laugh, saying," alright, that's got rid of the silliness. I could not resist it! If you pay me in silver coin I'll accept five pounds weight of coins each year in advance. I am happy for your employees to live on the first floor."

Gustav steps into the conversation. Freya knows she must allow Gustav to conclude the deal.

"Olag, we accept your proposal. I will call by tomorrow to pay you and then we'll start installing racking and storage platforms before moving our stock in. We have not got any staff yet, but we'll introduce you to them in due time."

Gustav and Freya go to the interim storage warehouse to check the condition of the bales of cloth and sacks of wool. They discuss what they need to do to set up the business. They know that confirmation to Dag in Jorvic must wait until the weather improves in the spring. They agree that this is a good thing as it gives them time to get established and give a positive report to Dag.

Freya completes the stock check, finding that all is well, and suggests, "Let's go home and tell mother all about what we have achieved. I have high hopes of doing well with Karl."

Ranveya has been very busy too, meeting builders, and discussing designs for the house. She arranges separate accommodation to be incorporated so that the house has three private areas and a common area for eating. She expects regular visits from Dag and his family, so the third private area will be designed to receive guests.

On leaving the meeting with the builders she informs them, "please let me have amended drawings, details of materials, how long construction will take and your prices within a week."

The builders, having concluded early on that Ranveya will not be taken advantage of, reply, "of course, you can rely on us. We may need to consult with you during that time, though." Ranveya responds, "that's fine by me."

That evening they discuss all that has happened and agree that everything ready for them to proceed. They feel they have just enough money to achieve things, but they are in no doubt that they must start trading without any delay.

During the next two months they all work hard.

Gustav meets and employs a team to install the racking and storage platforms. The men are honest and work hard, having been recommended by Olag.

Ranveya has agreed all matters relating to construction and furnishings.

As the work on both activities continues, Gustav and Freya start trading as soon as the stock of wool and bales of cloth are transferred to the new location. The cloth is unusual and popular the local population, particularly in respect of designs, many of which are inspired by Freya when she was in Narvik and Jorvic. They discover very quickly that Karl has extensive connections as far afield as the Mediterranean. One of the prime imports is ivory and pottery and the export of cloth in exchange makes for profitable business.

They judge that they have more than enough stock to cover the business needs until the next shipment comes in the spring from Jorvic. Gustav must ensure that a message gets through to Dag confirming that everything in Caen is ready and has arranged for the first ship to sail for Jorvic to carry the message.

Freya decides she needs to take a rest as she has been working hard for months without a break. She walks to the edge of town to a beautiful tree shaded open area which is popular with inhabitants for recreation. She has visited there frequently to watch young families gather to chat and play.

Many a time Freya finds herself in a reverie wishing she could be like these families with Frode by her side. During each visit she becomes more and more certain that the reunion time is coming. The situation in Caen seems to be providing just the right environment for business and family advancement.

Today, as the weather is very mild for the time of year she decides to walk there to relax, via the marketplace, after her meeting with the trader. There is something about the atmosphere around her causing her to feel a thrill of expectation that today will be different.

CHAPTER SEVENTEEN

THE SEPARATION YEARS

FRODE ARRIVES IN CAEN

The sea crossing from Wexford is long and arduous. Frode is totally unfit for the hard-disciplined rowing when the wind is unfavourable. However, at this time of year there is plenty of wind, albeit not always coming from the right direction, so not a great deal of rowing is required.

Frode knows fear at sea, as most people do, and finds himself praying to the Nordic Gods for their support in his safety. He is confused as he has accepted Christianity. What he does not realise is that his belief in the Nordic Gods is so embedded in his mind that his acceptance of the new religion is incomplete.

Later, in much calmer waters as the ship approaches the Normandy coast, he thinks about this conflict and is not going to be intimidated by it. Religion does not bother him too much despite his sojourn in Glendalough.

The ship is rowed upriver to the port of Caen where it docks. Frode goes to Jarl asking, "what do you want me to do?"

"Help supervise the unloading. My agent is coming on board to confirm the warehousing arrangements for my cargo. When that is done, I will take you to meet my friend Hakon, and ask him to give you shelter until you make more permanent arrangements. I believe the idea is for you to work for a manufacturing jeweller. Hakon will know who they are and arrange introductions."

The unloading takes most of the day, with Frode helping crew members putting the cargo into horse drawn carts. When all cargo is unloaded, the ship is secured, and the crew disperse. Frode's personal goods are kept with other cargo in a warehouse pending his settling in.

Jarl and Frode walk out of the dock area away from the hustle and bustle, up a gentle hill to a quiet part of the town where the people are wealthy. On reaching Hakon's house they are greeted by several children and dogs who are in a high state of excitement, as Jarl is popular. The children gather round Jarl who has a large bag containing little presents which he drops into eager outstretched hands.

The weather is typical of a late autumn evening, calm and bright which gives everybody a chance to mingle outside and socialise. Jarl introduces

Frode to Hakon and his very beautiful wife, Ingrid.

After the introductions, Jarl, explains some of Frode's background and why he is with him.

Jarl continues and asks, "would you be able to provide Frode shelter until he finds permanent accommodation? He hopes to find employment as a maker of jewellery, as well as meeting people who might like to have him visit them as a storyteller"

"Of course, you may stay for as long as you need." replies Ingrid, reflecting the Viking code of hospitality.

Ingrid shows Frode to a room at the back of the house which is reserved for guests. Frode concludes that the size of the house indicates that the family are successful traders. Later, he discovers that the wealth is based on slaves, which he cannot abide.

Jarl and Frode are invited to join the family in their meal, with Hakon stating, "you must tell us a story afterwards."

"That would be a pleasure."

Ingrid, as she is laying out the meal, wonders, "would you mind if I invited some friends to listen to you?"

"I am happy with that."

For the next hour they all enjoy their meal, chattering and catching up with gossip. Hakon introduces Frode and Jarl to a particularly strong ale which he brews himself.

While Jarl consumes several horns with relish, Frode is mindful of the need to remain sober for later When the meal is over Astrid sends two of the younger children to neighbours to invite them to come to hear a new storyteller. There is much excitement as Vikings love stories; this love has not been lost during their long period of settlement in Normandy.

Hakon and Ingrid's house's main room can accommodate up to twenty people and in a short while the room is full.

When everybody has settled down, Hakon addresses the guests.

"May I introduce my friend Jarl whom many of you have met before and Frode who comes from Narvik. Frode is going to settle here and become a maker of jewellery when he persuades someone to employ him."

Frode steps forward, saying, "I thank Ingrid and Hakon for their warm welcome and hospitality. I have been asked to tell you a story tonight, so I am going to tell you about part of my childhood in Narvik."

He stops, looking around the room, asks," do any of you originate from Norway?" A few hands are raised. "Are you mainly from Denmark?" There is a general murmur of agreement.

"In that case, as my story is centred on northern Norway, I will set the scene by describing the geography of the area and then go from there." There is an air of anticipation as Frode describes the beauty of the Narvik area and then holds his audience spellbound as he speaks of the children's acting out stories he created in collaboration with his friend Freya. He tells, too, of the prophesy.

Frode takes over an hour to tell his story and when he finishes there is a sustained period of applause.

There is a lot of discussion among the audience until one member poses a question." What has happened about the prophesy?"

Frode replies, "nothing yet. It may be that it will be here in Caen that the prophesy will come true. I feel it might do."

The questioner, reflecting the thoughts of many in the audience, comments, "would you let us know if it does?"

Frode, with wry grin, "you will be the first to know- after Freya, of course!" This brings a ripple of laughter.

The evening continues with singing and drinking in the traditional Viking style. Eventually the guests drift back to their homes but not before a number speak to Frode wondering if he would visit their houses regularly to entertain their families and guests. They offer to pay him, and he quickly agrees prices. Whilst the payments will never enough to live on, they will be a good supplement to his earnings as a jeweller. He is happy to have regular opportunities to do what he loves most.

The following day Hakon suggests that Frode comes with him to the slave market where many slaves, sent from the large island off the mainland, will be up for sale. Frode, who hates slavery, is reluctant to go, but not to be ungracious he agrees to go along.

The slave market, as in Wexford, is in a part of the harbour well away from the general area.

On arrival, Frode is appalled by the sight of men women and children chained together. They are all apathetic. He is about to leave when he becomes aware of a young woman slave staring at him, with lust in her eyes. He is unnerved and turns away from her stare. He then moves quickly over to where Hakon is bargaining hard for a group of male slaves. Hakon fails to strike a deal, losing out to a friend, who comments, "drinking hard last night, were you?"

Frode is thinking hard. I must get away from here.

CHAPTER EIGHTEEN
THE SEPARATION YEARS

FRODE SETTLES IN CAEN

As Frode drifts away from the horror of the slave market he is depressed. Even the glorious spring day does not lift his spirits, as he wishes he had never left the simple and clean life he enjoyed in Narvik. As his senses are assailed by the noise and bustle as he enters the marketplace, he realizes that he must accept Caen and its people as they really are and not as he would wish them to be.

As he wanders aimlessly around the stalls, he notices that there are children around. He has an idea. Maybe I can cheer myself up by telling the children a story.

He calls out, "children, would you like to hear a story?"

Within minutes he is surrounded by a horde of grubby little urchins with eager faces and sparkling eyes. Frode thinks this will be a new experience for them.

He invites the children," come on then, let's all sit down and I'll tell you about funny and mischievous little people I met in a beautiful land far across the sea."

As he starts his story, more and more children gather round together with some adults. He pauses for a minute or two to allow the audience to settle down. In an air of excitement

Frode sets the scene.

"In the beautiful country I have just come from there live little creatures called fairies, who are usually well behaved, and pixies, who are not usually well behaved. The story I am going to tell you is about the tricks the pixies play on the fairies and how the fairies get their own back. You see, fairies are little people who can fly, but the pixies cannot."

He draws little sketches in the earth of different types of fairies and pixeys which the children adore. One child asks, "can I draw some too?"

"Of course," replies Frode.

The child draws some pictures, displaying remarkable talent for small child, and the other children applaud her efforts. Frode wonders if there is a chance he could develop her skills, bur decides to let the matter lie for the moment.

Frode weaves a tale of the characters having lots of fun playing games and tricks on in each other at a fast and furious pace. The story lasts for half an hour during which the children are entranced.

When he finishes the children jump up and down, enthusiastically shouting, "Can we have more?"

Frode, thrilled by the response, and feeling that the gloom which had descended on him earlier has lifted, replies, "I'll be here tomorrow."

The children wander away, chattering happily.

One of the adults, who has been standing on the fringe of the group, goes over to Frode and introduces himself," I am Harald and I was in the audience last night. I think you are a fantastic storyteller. However, I'd like to talk to you about your experience as a jewellery maker as I own a small business here."

Frode, surprised that he could be about to find employment so quickly, replies, "I was trained by an experienced jeweller in Ireland and I believe I have the experience and the skills to be useful to you. I have brought some samples of my work with me."

Harald, sensing he has found someone who can help him expand his business, says, "come with me to my workshop over there," pointing to a building across the marketplace.

Frode happily walks with Harald, through the crowds of people, and on arrival at the workshop he is immediately impressed with scale of the business and the sense of industry displayed by the two employees. Frode stops many times to talk to the employees, who are proud to show what they are doing.

Harald questions Frode closely about his experience and is particularly interested in his design skills. He feels that Frode would be an asset to his business but says nothing yet.

Harald suggests," Frode, would you come back tomorrow and bring your samples?"

"Of course, I'd love to, but I may get waylaid by the children!"

Harald comments," If you come to work for me, you'll need to find the time outside your working hours. Also, I am a difficult man to please."

"I understand; there will be no problem, I assure you."

Frode takes his leave saying," see you tomorrow morning."

As Frode walks back to Hakon's house, it starts to rain heavily and Frode is soaked to the skin. Nothing, however, is going to dampen his spirits. On his arrival, Ingrid shows motherly concern, "you must change into dry clothes immediately.

The story you are bursting to tell me can wait. Anyway, Hakon is not home yet."

At this moment, Hakon arrives with rainwater streaming down his face muttering darkly that he is fed up of being wet. He, too, is instructed by Ingrid to get changed.

Ingrid has prepared a meal of assorted smoked fish, meat in the Viking style, complemented by some of Hakon's ale.

The family sit down for their meal and they all describe the things they had done during the day. The two children are fascinated by the idea of Frode telling stories to children and ask him to tell them one. Ingrid agrees to that but only after the meal has been eaten.

After the meal is over Frode sits with the children and tells them an edited version of the morning story, which thrills them. They ask lots of questions which enables Frode to weave fantastic descriptions of clothes worn by fairies and pixeys, together with descriptions of the fairies' flying skills.

Hakon and Frode continue the evening drinking, while Ingrid settles the children down. Frode tells of his meeting with Harald and the prospect of working with him.

Hakon comments, "it was not a joke last night, Harald is a very awkward fellow."

"I did not get that impression today as Harald spoke freely of his business and his plans for expansion, although he did say he was a hard man to please."

"Well you can only try to get on with him, provided, of course, he offers you a job!" says Hakon scowling.

Frode has a feeling that there have been problems between the two of them in the past.

Hakon, pouring more ale into his drinking horn, takes a mighty gulp and, beginning to slur his words, says, "tomorrow is a major market day and Ingrid wants to go down to the market early to see what bargains she can find. You can be sure she will gossip most of the time. The stallholders live in fear of her, as I do," says Hakon grinning broadly.

Frode eventually retires to bed as Hakon says, "good luck for tomorrow."

In the morning, after a light breakfast Ingrid sets off to market with the children. Hakon goes to meet a trader and Frode collects his jewellery samples, then sets off to see Harald.

The weather is threatening, with a stiff wind and dark clouds scudding across a grey sky. Frode strides quickly to Harald's workshop, head down into the wind. He feels that he is a about to get close to Freya.

On reaching the workshop Frode and Harald sit down to examine and discuss Frode's jewellery's designs and quality.

Harald critically appraises Frode's workmanship.

Turning to Frode he says, "I like what I see, and I'd like to employ you, primarily as a designer. I can offer you living accommodation at the back in your own private area. My other employees live there too."

They agree employment terms and Frode is to start work the next day.

Frode returns to Hakon and Ingrid's house, packs up his belongings and waits for their return in the late afternoon.

During the evening meal he tells them what has happened and explains he is to move into his new living quarters the next day.

"May I thank you both for your hospitality. I shall never forget your generosity and I hope we can remain friends,

Hakon and Ingrid are happy to agree.

Frode says to the children, "I am leaving tomorrow to work for a man who makes jewellery. I will be in the marketplace most days telling stories to children. I would love to see you there if mum and dad have no objections."

Ingrid, to the delight of the children says, "yes."

During the next month Frode settles in. As expected Harald proves a hard taskmaster, but Frode is not easily upset and, as the weeks go by, they form a respectful relationship. They exchange ideas on design in a spirit of harmony. The result is the production of designs of great beauty. Some are simple, and some are complex. They prove to be popular with buyers and sales start to increase noticeably.

One day, a couple turn up looking for work. They explain to Harald that they have recently arrived in Caen. The introduce themselves as Alfgerirra and Eira.

In the conversation it turns out that Eira is a talented artist; she does some sketches of jewellery in front of Harald which, although quite different from Frode's, matches his quality.

Eira says," I have no skills but I am willing to learn."

Harald ponders for a moment, looks at Frode who raises an eyebrow. Then he says, "ok I'll give you both a trial."

Frode continues to tell his children's stories most mornings before he starts work. From time to time, in the evenings, he has invitations to present stories at dinner parties and social gatherings.

He decides to devote one or two of his storytelling sessions to explain how he creates his stories and how the children can contribute their ideas. This leads to his realising how creative some children can be, given the opportunity.

One day, as he finishes his stories for the morning, he has a feeling that something dramatic is about to happen. He shakes his head to clear it and then walks to his workshop.

CHAPTER NINETEEN

THE REUNION IN CAEN, NORMANDY.

It is market day in central Caen. The noise is incredible as vendors call out to entice customers to their stalls. There is nothing that cannot be bought and sold here.

Hucksters, beggars, and servants of the rich from the nearby large houses are all milling about with everything happening; people are examining goods and bargaining. Musicians are playing next to food stalls offering exotic foods as well as staples. Children and animals are running around, getting under people's feet. The scene is chaotic and exciting.

Frode is ambling about, taking a break from his jewellery workshop, observing the sheer vibrancy of the scene, looking for ideas for stories for the children who flock to his daily story telling. He has changed his working clothes for a dark blue cape over a leather jerkin, trousers, and boots. His hair is tied back. He cuts a fine figure, drawing admiring glances from many women. As he strolls past a flower seller's stall he is startled by the sight of a beautiful woman walking just ahead of him. She is dressed in the style of a Viking lady of wealth, wearing a long green woollen cloak, with a shawl of cream coloured wool, offsetting perfectly her long hair. In a flash he knows who she is; she is his long-lost childhood love, Freya!

Freya, looking behind her as a small child collides with her legs, sees Frode and knows instantly that she has found the one person for whom she has never lost her love. She is, however, hesitant to show recognition, as her thoughts race through her mind in wild confusion. Then it is as though a dam has burst as her feelings overwhelm her. She turns and walks slowly forward in a daze, her arms outstretched to him, as tears stream down her face.

Frode is completely taken aback by the intensity of the moment, not sure how to handle the situation, which is completely outside his experience. However, Freya's beauty, and the way she walks towards him, remove any inhibitions and he gives way to the sheer emotional magic. He has, over the years, been constantly aware of her, but her closeness now has unleashed what can only be a desire to capture her and love her. He takes her gently in his arms to hold her close. She is still crying as they continue to embrace in a total immersion in each other's senses.

Passers-by are caught up in the powerful vibes coming from the couple, sensing that they are witnessing something very special, not just an ordinary couple meeting and embracing. They cannot know that a prophesy is being fulfilled before their eyes-they can but wonder. They do not speak as Frode takes Freya's hand and gently leads her slowly to the house where he composes his stories and has his jewellery workshop. He knows he has found the most powerful love story he could devise.

Freya, reluctant to enter Frode's home, whispers in his ear, "I know a peaceful place a short distance from here where we can sit and talk."

"I agree," replies Frode, "but first I must collect something from the house. Bear with me for a moment and wait for me."

He disappears into the house, finds the brooch he had made in Wexford, and puts it in a pocket of his jerkin. They stroll, hand in hand, until they reach a secluded area of grass surrounded by shrubs and trees with a slope leading down to a small lake. A host of water birds, mainly different varieties of ducks, are busy feeding or chasing each other in great exuberance. It is normally a place where children play, but today there are few of them about as there is a troupe of players entertaining children in the marketplace.

The weather is dry warm and sunny which is a major improvement over the previous few weeks.

Maybe the Norse Gods want to make the reunion, so long awaited, something magical, in a place of peace. They sit down on the grass, kissing passionately so that the world seems to stop as they are totally absorbed in the magic of the moment.

"Our reunion!" cries Freya, "it has just come true, hasn't it?"

Frode, seeing the vision clearly agrees," yes, it has!"

There is a short period of silence as each contemplates the significance of what has just happened. Then Freya, looking a little wistful, says, "I have a problem as I have to see some merchants about setting up trading deals as I work with my father in his trading business. Yet there is so much to talk about and having found you I never want to leave you."

Frode, still in a state of confusion, and simply wanting to hold Freya close to him, reaches into his pocket and says, "We have been apart for so long that another day won't matter! However, I cannot wait, as I want to give you this brooch which I made for you when I was in Wexford in Ireland, as token of my never- forgotten love for you."

Freya is overwhelmed and hesitantly tries to fix it to her cape with shaking fingers. Frode moves close to help her and between them they fix it in place. In that instant both hear the voice of the Goddess Freya.

Her voice, clear, yet intense, whispers, "I have endowed this brooch with powers to protect its owner from injury or death, other than from old age, for ever. It must be passed to future generations through the male line of the family dynasty you will create. It will survive tragedies and misfortune and ensure the family survival, one way or another, into the distant future. I cannot foretell what that future will be, but I can, through the power vested in this brooch ensure that the family will never die out."

Frode whispers, "My love, we are truly chosen of the Gods. I know we are both Christian, but I do hope that the Christian God will support the favour placed upon us by the Nordic Gods and allow us to honour it."

Freya, weeping in sheer happiness," I agree. Let's now go forward and meet our destiny."

They kiss tenderly and agree to meet at the same place the following day.

Freya, taking a deep breath, draws Frode to her, kisses him long and slowly, "till tomorrow, my love."

She leaves and walks slowly towards the street.

When she meets the merchant, she realises she is in no emotional state to get involved in trade negotiations and resolves to make the meeting a social one only.

She explains that information she needs from Jorvic has not reached her. She persuades the merchant to wait until she has the information. He knows that the outline deals put to him by Freya's father are very attractive and there is nothing to lose by waiting, so he accepts the situation.

Freya is now torn between rushing back to see Frode and returning home. However, she realises that Frode is likely to have returned to where he works and decides to go home to tell her parents and seek Ranveya's advice.

When Freya gets home she is in a state of great excitement. "Mother," she exclaims, "it's happened!"

"What's happened?"

"The prophesy has come true. I've just met Frode in the marketplace"

Ranveya takes Freya in her arms, saying, "so, at last, after all this time, the Gods have honoured their promise."

Freya, still unable to speak coherently, describes what happened at the meeting.

"Frode gave me this brooch which he made when he was in Ireland."

Ranveya admires it and senses that it is imbued with some special powers.

Freya continues, "when Frode was pinning it on my cloak, Goddess Freya spoke to us both saying that the brooch would protect its owner and it was to be handed down far into the future through the male line of the family to be created by us both."

"I know we are both Christian; he told me about some of his involvement with a monastery in Ireland. However, I feel drawn still to the old Nordic Gods and would want to continue to commit to them."

"I don't think our priests would be too happy with that, but you must follow your own conscience provided Frode is in full agreement."

Ranveya continues, "when you feel the time is right bring Frode home to see us. It would be wonderful to see him again."

At that moment Gudrun comes into the house and is immediately caught up in the women's excitement. Freya has calmed down and explains what has happened.

"That's great news," says Gudrun, "but what did the merchant have to say at your meeting?"

"Oh dear, I was in such an emotional state that I asked him to wait until another day or so. I did lie by claiming that not all the information we required had arrived from Jorvic."

Gudrun showing some anger," do you realise how important these contracts will be to us? You must not allow personal matters to interfere with business."

Ranveya, rushing to calm things down, "our meal is ready. We should discuss the situation calmly while we are eating and decide what we should do. We must never forget the prophesy and accept that Freya and Frode are the chosen couple."

"I apologise for being so thoughtless," he says as Freya gives him a hug. "I will remember my duties, I promise," replies Freya.

They decide that the best plan is for Freya and Frode to have a courtship in the Viking tradition and see if they really do want to marry.

Gunter, just before retiring to bed, says, "Freya, mother and I always have your happiness at heart. Follow it, we will support you. Do not work tomorrow but try to meet Frode. You have both got years of stories to share. I doubt a day will be enough!"

Freya finds it impossible to sleep as her mind churns all night with a mixture of joy and fear. She knows her life is going to change dramatically.

Next morning dawns sunny but chilly. She eats a light breakfast and takes great care in selecting her clothes, focusing on a long green woollen cloak to which she has fixed her new brooch. The result is dazzling with Ranveya commenting, "you will enchant Frode. I do hope he will be worthy of you."

"Oh, I am very sure of that," she says, walking jauntily out the door.

Meantime, Frode also has had a restless night and is not sure what to do in the morning as he realises that he did not arrange a time to meet Freya. He is in no mood to go to the workshop, so he decides to go to the marketplace and find some children to talk to. He, like Freya, decides to dress well, wearing a leather jerkin and dark maroon coloured cloak.

As he is telling a story about Irish "little people" to the children he sees Freya approaching. Her beauty and bearing take his breath away and he stutters to a halt, puzzling the children. Freya stops at the edge of the group, offers Frode a dazzling smile, and says, "please continue. I'd like to hear your story too."

Frode continues the story and when he has finished he tells the children," that's all for today, I will see you again tomorrow." One small girl with a degree of confidence belying her age, looks intensely at Freya and enquires sweetly, "who are you? You are so beautiful."

"I am Frode's future wife."

With a delighted expression on her face the girl races off to tell her friends, then returns," can we come to your wedding please?" Both are nonplussed by her audacity.

"We'll see what we can do," replies Freya with a broad smile.

Freya moves to sit down by Frode's side. The weather has become warmer, so they are happy to stay there for the moment. As always the scene is noisy and full of busy people.

Frode is shy and tongue-tied while Freya is bright and talkative. Slowly, Frode relaxes and the two chatter away non-stop, both rushing to tell of their adventures since they were last together.

Frode starts off by saying, "I will tell you in more detail later of my wanderings and adventures in and around Dyflin, Glendalough and Waterford in Ireland-such a beautiful island out to the west."

Freya then offers," and I will tell you of my adventures in Narvik after you left, then in Jorvic and here in Caen. I must tell you that rarely did a day go by when I did not think of you and wonder where and how you were. I could not respond to any approaches by men because you were always my lost love. Only the Gods' prophesy sustained me."

Frode responding, a little ruefully, "I have been the same, although I must admit I did weaken once, and I was so conscious stricken I felt unhappy."

Freya, chuckling softly. "what, only once?" Frode deems it wise to let the remark pass.

After a period of general chatter, Freya, looking very thoughtful, poses the inevitable question.

"Where do we go from here?"

Frode, taking Freya's hands in his, asks, "will you marry me?"

"Yes, my love, as soon as possible!"

They become aware of a presence, look up and see the small group of children that Frode was talking to earlier. The children are standing watching.

Frode, in a moment of inspiration, declares, "please sit down and I will tell you a wonderful love story. Freya, here, will join me."

The children sit down quietly while they are told of the Frode and Freya's childhood, their adventures leading to their reunion. The children are entranced especially when Freya shows them her brooch. They ask to see it more closely and Freya passes it round. The little girl who earlier had asked to be invited to the wedding exclaimes," oooooooh, my hand is tingling!"

"that is because it has magic powers," says Freya.

As the girl hands the brooch back, Freya wonders if the event has any significance.

At the end of the story everybody leaves the scene.

Frode and Freya walk hand in hand back to the marketplace knowing that they will go forward to meet their destiny.

CHAPTER TWENTY

FRODE AND FREYA MARRY

Frode and Freya meet many times in the evenings at Frode's house over the ensuing weeks, during which they make love, and tell the stories of their adventures after Frode had left Narvik. While they continue their work, they find time to stroll around the town, followed by a gaggle of children, stopping from time to time to tell the children a story. The children particularly love stories about mischievous Irish pixies.

Soon afterwards Freya's parents invite Frode to dine with them one evening. On arrival Frode is warmly welcomed by Gustav and Ranveya. Both are impressed with Frode's bearing and stylish dress. Ranveya does not missing the devilish twinkle in his eye.

There is so much to talk about that Ranveya must keep order. Freya is very relieved that Frode is accepted.

While Frode and Freya want to marry in the Viking way, it becomes clear after Ranveya has had a long discussion with Freya that this will not be possible. The communities in Normandy are long established Christian ones and a pagan ceremony would not be tolerated. If they were to proceed the whole family would be ostracised. Freya acccpts this and arrangements to organise the wedding are started.

Freya is unhappy that she and Frode are to miss being blessed by the Goddess Freya and resolves that this must be achieved. She also instinctively needs Freya's blessing so that she can conceive. She is much preoccupied by thoughts on how to achieve this. One day, as she takes a break from work, she wanders along the nearby riverbank bank. She feels drawn to a clump of trees and bushes and wanders over to look. Immediately on seeing a small clearing she realises that this will be the place where she and Forde will seek the blessing in what will be an intensely private and emotional moment. She kneels to pray to the Goddess in supplication.

"Please, when we come here after our marriage in the Christian form, grace us with your blessing for a long and fruitful life, and help us establish the dynasty you have foretold."

Freya has a feeling she has been heard and walks to Frode's workshop to tell him. She waits for him to finish working on a piece and is fascinated by the delicacy of his work, his patience, and skill.

When he has finished he goes to her and holds her tight while she explains what she has arranged.

"What a wonderful idea," he whispers in her ear. "We can keep faith with the old Gods."

As the weeks roll by Ranveya, Freya and friends and neighbours combine to set up the wedding ceremony and the celebrations.

The local priest meets with Frode and Freya and is very interested in Frode's time in Glendalough and how the monastery operates. He has no idea that they still cling to the old Gods, nor will he ever find out.

In the build-up to the wedding, Freya continues to work in the trading business. Gustav suggests to Frode that he could join him in the business, especially after Freya has children. They discuss it but Frode prefers to stand alone in providing for his future family and explains his view to Gustav who accepts Frode's decision. He is making a good living selling his jewellery through his employer, in a special arrangement which works well.

The wedding day arrives, and the ceremony is carried out in the Christian tradition to which neither objects. They quietly offer prayers to Goddess Freya as they retire to the place reserved for prayer and contemplation in the church.

Afterwards, there is a boisterous party at Gustav and Ranveya's house, including the children who form much of Frode's story telling audience. There is one little girl who is beside herself with joy.

Frode and Freya expect to live in Frode's little house at the back of the jewellery workshop. As the celebrations end, Gustav calls for silence, which takes some time to achieve.

Eventually, he addresses the crowd, "we are all going for a short walk, led by Ranveya and myself, followed by Freya and Frode," who exchange puzzled looks. They shrug their shoulders and follow Freya's parents outside.

As the crowd walks happily singing and cavorting about they attract a sizable crowd, many of whom are children.

They arrive outside a large single storey new house built of wattle and daub with a thatched roof. Gustav and Ranveya walk to the front door as Freya and Frode are still uncomprehending.

They hold out their arms to the newly-weds, saying, "come, accept our wedding present. Be happy here and bring up your family in the way foretold so many years ago."

Freya and Frode go forward, Freya with tears streaming down her face; they embrace their parents, turn to the crowd and amid cheers and ribald comments, wave and move inside. There is much singing and dancing while the couple explore their new home. It is spacious, having a family gathering room, cooking, and eating area and four self- contained sleeping areas. There is no furniture, but Freya realises that they are to furnish the house as they wish.

They go outside to tumultuous applause and cries of, "let's see, let's see!" They stand aside and wave their friends in to see the interior.

Freya picks up the little girl who had asked to come to the wedding and gives her a special tour, much to her great delight.

As the festivities continue, Freya whispers to her mother, "we must slip away to make our devotions to Goddess Freya. We shall return as soon as we can. Perhaps you could dissuade people from following us!"

"I will try, but I suggest you take a circuitous route to where you are going!"

Freya and Frode slip away unnoticed and go to the glade that Freya had found.

Together they kneel, and holding hands, call to Freya, "bless us we pray and make our union fruitful as foretold. Protect our dynasty in whatever form it may take. We shall worship you despite the changes in religion which are taking place."

A warm glow suffuses the glade and they both feel great comfort and strength flow through them. As the glow fades they embrace and then lie together to make love. Goddess Freya ensures that a child is conceived in that special place and arranges with the senior Goddess Frigg to strengthen the protection.

A little while later they re-join the festivities and after the revellers finally return to their homes, they retire to Frode's home.

Frode is now so busy that he ceases to tell stories at adult party gatherings, which were not a great success anyway. He is far more at ease with children and no longer needs earn money from storytelling.

As Freya's pregnancy develops smoothly, she is certain that Goddess Freya is watching over her. Frode, too, is loving and attentive.

CHAPTER TWENTY-ONE

THE FULFILMENT

Frode and Freya move furniture and all their belongings into their new house. They continue to do their work and intersperse their activities with the morning storytelling for the children, who follow them around constantly. Freya now joins in the storytelling; the children still love the stories about mischievous Irish pixies.

The trouble is that the children cannot resist re-enacting the pixie stories, but most parents are content that the children are happy.

It is a happy time for Frode and Freya as they discover the joy of being soulmates and eagerly await the birth of their first child. They are surrounded by family and friends who realise that they are a special couple.

In due time Freya gives birth to a boy. She senses that Goddesses Frig and Freya are there watching over her.

Freya presents the baby to Frode who, kissing her very tenderly, takes the child, well wrapped up in a woollen shawl, outside to show him to the waiting friends and family. "I give you Olaf!" he declares.

There is a great roar of approval. The cry is,"Let the party begin!" Once the festivities die down Freya makes it clear that she wants them to have a happy ordinary family life yet preparing Olaf and any later children for a future which will be anything but ordinary.

Over the years Frode works very hard in the jewellery business, eventually taking over the business when the owner dies. He continues his morning storytelling with the children.

In a five- year period two more children are born, a boy, Gustav and a girl, Iona. Both are healthy, but Freya's health deteriorates after the difficult birth of Iona.

Shortly after Iona is born Freya's parents die within months of each other and Frode and Freya take over the trading business.

Frode, aware that he has no trading skills, is unhappy about giving up his business, saying," we must discuss plans for the future and agree a strategy. So that the prophesy can come true it is essential we get things right."

"I agree. I have an idea which should solve the problem. We must not give up such a good income."

"What is your idea?"

"Well, I need to look after the children and run our house.

After Iona's birth I am not as fit as I used to be. Suppose we ask our two best employees, Petr and Andrew to take over the running of the trading business in return for, say, a twenty percent stake each and still retain their salaries. I can, with your help, deal with accounting and sales."

"That's a brilliant idea, provided you are fit enough."

"If I cannot continue in the future then we will face that."

Frode is happy that he can continue with his business. However, he has concern for the future, as his children have many years to go before reaching maturity as it is always possible that the children may want to seek their fortunes elsewhere.

"Freya, I think we should do the same for the jewellery business."

"I agree. Do you have anyone in mind?"

"Actually, I think I do. Do you remember Halvar and Eira. I believe they are working on a farm not too far away."

"Yes, I do. I think they could well be suitable. Let's see if we can find them."

They both put out enquiries in the marketplace and in the area of the display and sale of farmers' produce.

Some days later Eira calls on Frode's workshop claiming, "hello again, I believe you are looking for us."

"Yes, thank you for coming to see me. Freya and I would like to meet you and Halvar as we have a proposal to put to you."

"I am intrigued! When and where shall we meet?"

Frode, with a charming smile which disarms Eira, "how about tomorrow at 10 o'clock?"

"OK, I think that will be fine, but Halvar will need to agree time off with our employer."

Frode returns home, informing Freya, "I have met Eira, and all going well, they will meet me at the workshop."

Freya is unhappy with this idea. "I want to be there but I cannot leave the children." Can you bring them here?"

Frode agrees. He is desperately concerned for Freya. He loves her so much that he cannot bear the thought for one moment of losing her after waiting so long and tells her, "I love you so much I am frightened I lose you. I will give you anything you want."

"Just love me and allow me to be part of everything you do. Remember we have a duty to prepare our children for their future. We are soulmates."

Frode replies, "the Gods have given us a task and we are being granted a wonderful marriage to help make the children be influential in spheres still to be revealed to us. However, the Gods are devious enough not to reveal the future while we are still alive. We must trust them, otherwise there would be no point." The next day Halvar and Eira meet Frode as arranged and they go to meet Freya at Frode's house. The reunion is an emotional one for Freya as she has an affinity with Elvira dating from the voyage from England.

After catching up on what happened after they parted, Frode goes on to explain, "we are running two businesses and we want Freya to concentrate on running our trading business. That leaves my jewellery business. I feel that I should have someone running the business alongside me so that when I die it can continue if the children want to be involved. If they do not, then the whole business would become owned by my partners."

Both Halvar and Eira are stunned by Frode's proposition.

They are concerned about their lack of knowledge, with Halvar exclaiming, "we know nothing at all about the business!"

"Neither did I three years ago. I learned and so can you because I will teach you," replies Frode.

"I will pay you what you are earning now and give you accommodation at the back of the workshop. At the end of each year for four years I will give you a ten per cent share of the business, assuming you do well and wish to continue. If you decide to leave before the end of the fourth year the ownership of your share will be sold back to the children via an adult willing to act as guardian. In due time our children will inherit the remaining sixty percent. If none of them want their shares then the business will become completely yours. Full details of shall be written down and lodged with the town's ruling Council."

Frode continues, with Freya nodding approval, "While you are thinking please come to visit the workshop, watch operations and ask questions."

Halvar and Eira are enthusiastic and they all stay together for several hours talking of many things.

Before they leave Eira spends time with Freya and the children. Freya decides to confide in Eira, telling her about the prophesy, at the end of which Eira says, "what a wonderful story. To be chosen of the Gods must be an incredible experience."

Then it is agreed that a meeting late the next day will take place at the workshop.

The next day is an ordinary day in the life of Frode and Freya. On his way to the workshop Frode is mobbed by children. He leads them to the corner of the marketplace which has become known as "The place of fantasies and adventure."

Here Frode regales his audience with part two of a long story about elves and pixies. Frode has invented the story which allows him to let his and the children's imagination fly.

Later, towards evening, Halvar and Eira arrive at Frode's workshop, saying," we have discussed your proposition and agree that you are offering a wonderful opportunity and we would like to see and learn more."

Frode, delighted to hear the news, says, "that is fantastic, so let's tour the workshop, meet some of the working team and we can go back to my house to have a chance for Freya and me to answer your questions."

The tour is long and detailed, with Halvar and Eira posing a stream of questions. Afterwards they return to Frode's house where Freya has prepared a meal. Discussion goes on well into the night and they decide that Halvar and Eira stay overnight so that the whole plan be reviewed in the morning.

The next morning, after breakfast, since the weather is warm and sunny, they all sit outside while the children are playing with neighbours' children.

Halvar and Eira say, "we are happy with the proposal you have made and would like to join you as soon we sort matters out with our employer. Frode, reflecting Freya's pleasure as well as his, says, "this is wonderful. I am sure we have all made the right decision. So, let's get on with it as soon as possible."

Three weeks later Halvar and Eira start work.

Freya feels she needs spiritual guidance and asks Frode to come with her to the glade where they spent some time after their wedding.

"Frode," she says, "I know we are both Christians, but I cannot turn my back on our old Gods, particularly Freya and I want to commune with her so that I can be assured that she will watch over our descendants."

Frode, conscious of his great love for Freya, and reading her mind, "I agree. Let's go to the glade now."

They take the children with them and walk, hand in hand, to the glade. When they reach it, they see that nothing has changed. The sun is shining through the trees casting light and shadow all around. The children seem to sense the solemnity of the scene and become subdued without understanding why.

As they kneel together, with their children cuddled into them, Freya calls to Goddess Freya," hear us please. We are unsure that we are following the path set before us, especially that for our children who you see before you."

There is a stirring of a light breeze through the leaves of the trees and the light dims slightly. Freya appears as a vision before them. She speaks," we, Gods of the Viking race, are pleased that you have kept your faith in us. I have watched over you as I promised and you and Frode are bringing up your children in the manner we hoped you would. You see that your lovely children are not frightened by me as I have instilled in them a love of me and my fellow Gods.

We shall never abandon them or their descendants, even though they will not be aware of our protection."

"Thank you, Freya," says Frode, in awe of what has just happened.

The children, releasing a burst of pent up energy, chase around like mad things. Iona is too young to join in but chortles happily while in Freya's arms.

Feeling elated and comforted the family returns home.

CHAPTER TWENTY- TWO

THE FAMILY MATURES

During the next few years Frode and Freya work hard to educate and care for their children, while continuing to run their businesses. The partners brought in to help have succeeded in their roles to the extent that both businesses have grown substantially.

Sadly, Freya's health continues to deteriorate to the point where she is no longer fit to continue running the business, relying more and more on Petr and Andrew to take the load.

Frode is desperately concerned for Freya and spends as much time as he can caring for her. Eventually he realises that Freya's life is ebbing away as she loses weight and seems to be suffering from a form of wasting disease. He meets with Halvar and Eira and says to them, "Freya is dying, and I must be with her and care for her. I'd like you two to run the business until such times as I can return."

Both agree immediately, "we are honoured that you trust us. We will let not you down. Freya is lucky to have someone like you to care for her. May we call by from time to time to see her?"

"Of course, we would both welcome that." Frode returns to the house and explains what he has done, "I love you so much I cannot bear the thought of losing you. I will stay with you day and night."

"My love I thank you, for I fear that I do not have long before I pass over. The pain is increasing every day. Bless them, the children understand and have promised to be worthy of us."

A week later Goddess Freya appears to Freya, saying, "you have done everything we expected of you. I can tell you of your family's future and of the power and influence they achieve."

The Goddess then outlines the family's influence on world affairs for the following thousand years. As Freya listens, the pain starts to recede.

Freya is in Frode's arms, with the children sitting nearby. She knows her time has come as the pain goes and she feels warm and calm. She looks up into Frode's eyes and whispers," goodbye my love. Thank you for giving me such lovely children and happiness. I know the dynasty is about to be established. Look after the children, they are the future as foretold." Freya then quietly slips away as Frode weeps.

Freya is buried according to Christian ritual, but Frode has quietly placed a piece of wood in her coffin, inscribed with runes, beseeching the Goddess to take Freya to her ancestors according to Viking rites.

Freya's funeral is attended by so many friends and other associates that the church cannot accommodate them all.

After the ceremony and everybody departs Frode sits down and tell his children the greatest story he will ever tell-that of the prophesy.

As Frode speaks the children sit spell bound and when he has finished he is inundated with questions, most of which he can answer.

Each child is interested in how the prophesy will work for them.

Frode answers, "the Gods have not yet revealed all the details and may never do. All I know is that you will be presented with opportunities. See and seize them!"

Frode stops for a moment while he opens a pouch which he has round his neck. He shows them the brooch which he keeps there since Freya died, saying, with tears in his eyes," I made this brooch for your mother when I was wandering Ireland."

"Where's Ireland they chorused?"

"I will tell you after I have finished! This brooch is vested with special protection powers by the Viking Goddess Freya after whom you mother was named. I want to set a vital task for you and your descendants.

The Gods expect that the brooch and its protection will pass down the generations to be worn by the wife of the oldest son, or the next oldest in the event that the oldest does not marry or has no children. Gustav is charged with custody of the brooch which will remain with his descendants unless it moves to another branch of the family. Other branches will be protected too but they may not be aware of it. I hope that the story will pass down the generations even though the family is now Christian. The old Gods will survive albeit quietly behind the scenes to honour the promise.

You wanted to know where Ireland is. It is a beautiful and fertile island way out to the west beyond the horizon. There is a large Viking settlement called Dyflyn. I spent many happy years in Ireland on my way here."

The children run out to play, chattering about what they have heard. Gustav, however, is troubled as he is unsure how to handle the responsibility. He goes back into the house only to find Frode sitting holding the brooch and whispering," oh Freya, how I miss you. I will join you soon. Two separations are unbearable."

Gustav quietly turns and slips outside.

During the next six years Frode devotes time to ensuring his children get a practical education and are offered the opportunities to learn about the two businesses.

While Gustav shows little interest in trading, Olaf finds his purpose in life is trading and so devotes his time to developing his skills. Petr and Andrew are his mentors as Frode grows older and plays a lesser part in the business. There are signs that he is actually missing Freya so much that he is neglecting his health. He has the comfort of seeing his children grow to adulthood and quietly gives thanks to Goddess Freya for his having a happy and fruitful life. One night he prays to the goddess saying that he is tired and wants desperately to reunite with his beloved Freya.

The Goddess appears to him and says" you are right. Your time has come. As with Freya, the Gods are pleased with you and will now reveal to you the future of your family. It is a magnificent one."

She tells him of the future. When she has finished he gets out of bed, goes to his pouch and takes out the brooch. He leaves it on a table knowing that Gustav will take care of it and returns to bed.

He is overcome with peace and warmth. Then he sees Freya standing in their glade with her arms outstretched towards him, saying, "come to me my love."

CHAPTER TWENTY-THREE

GUSTAV'S PREPARATION

After the funeral Gustav retains the brooch as instructed by Frode for safekeeping.

The family meets and they agree that they accept that Olaf inherits the trading business, Gustav is uncertain what he wants to do, while Iona keeps house until she marries. She wants to be a farmer's wife. In addition, Halvar and Eira take over Frode's jewellery business.

Before the meeting ends, Gustav says, "please can we not forget our Viking gods who have encouraged our family to excel through the great and lasting love of our parents. I will have custody of the brooch our father made for mother and we should always remember the powers that Goddess Freya gave it. I know we are Christians, but we should try to remember our heritage for as long as it is possible. Let us now offer a prayer of thanksgiving to Goddess Freya."

All kneel, hold hands as Gustav intones, "Goddess Freya, we thank you for all you have done for our family. May we be always worthy of your trust."

Gustav finds that he always wants to be near horses, which are attracted to him too. He once visited the farm that Halvar and Eira worked at and watched horses being trained. He goes back to the farm, meets the farmer, and makes an agreement that he would labour on the farm in exchange for the use of a horse and training. It does not take long for Gustav to excel in several forms of horse riding.

One day a few years later a friend of the farmer, a cavalry officer in Duke William's army, calls by. He notices Gustav riding hard and mastering a series of high jumps and ditches.

The officer remarks to the farmer, "that young lad shows promise. Please keep an eye on him and train him hard. I will help pay for some of his training, provided you don't tell him. I will come back from time to time to see what progress he is making. If he proves really good enough I will recommend him to Duke William."

The farmer replies, "I am happy to oblige. Leave it to me. It would be an honour to provide a recruit to the Duke." During his horseriding Gustav is exhilarated by the speed of the horses and their power. He gets to know several influential people having connections with Duke William's hierarchy who come to the farm to view and buy horses. He hears stories of Duke William's excursions into neighbouring lands and decides he wants to join Duke Williams forces as a cavalryman. Duke William is told of a man who shows exceptional leadership and horsemanship skills and he orders Gustav to attend a celebratory banquet at his castle in Falaise. Gustav meets a cavalry officer called Henri who accompanies him to Falaise. On arrival Gustav is nervous beforehand, so Henri takes him on a horse-riding trip to distract him.

When the horses are being returned to stables, Gustav sees a striking looking girl of about his own age. "Watch it, that's Duke William's cousin. Leave her well alone!" observes Henri. As the girl smiles at him, Gustav is smitten. He is staying at Henri's house and will return there to get ready for the banquet.

As he sets off he hears a voice from the stables," Emma do hurry, or we will be late for the banquet." Emma scuttles inside with a sly backward glance, making Gustav go weak at the knees.

Duke William has strict rules about dress and Henri has to lend Gustav the appropriate dress. It is important that no-one outshines William.

They arrive at the banquet in William's castle in Falaise, a short distance from Caen. William is proud of the castle where he was born and likes to show it off, giving banquets in the great hall.

All guests are seated at long tables set below William's top table where a meal of various meats, fish, vegetables, and bread is served accompanied by copious amounts of ale.

Although Gustav is seated well down the room he sees Emma at top table and is entranced. Henri notices this and again warns him," be careful!" Gustav pretends not to hear. The evening progresses with boisterous singing, eating, and stories of military prowess. Each story grows more and more exaggerated as time goes on.

Gustav has a quiet smile to himself, but he recognises the camaraderie among the cavalry officers. He feels at home with them and resolves to join them if he can. In the turmoil he has forgotten that Duke William has summoned him to attend.

An aide comes bustling over and whispers in his ear," Duke William wishes to meet you now. Follow me."

Gustav follows the aide to the Duke's presence.

Duke William indicates that Gustav should sit next to him. Gustav is conscious of Emma being close and her watching him. Duke William looks at him with his piercing eyes and says," I have heard stories of your skills as a horseman and I am thinking it would be worth seeing how good you are. If you are, I will accept you into my cavalry for training and full evaluation. I have need of more officers. Report with Henri at my stables tomorrow morning at 7 o'clock. He will set you up with a horse and tack. Dismissed."

On his way back to his table he looks back and is disappointed to see that Emma is not there. His newfound friends have settled into a night's carousing, but Gustav thinks it wise to leave and get some sleep ready for the morning. He returns to Henri's quarters.

Next morning, he and Henri go to the Duke's stables where they find a hive of activity with all horses being prepared for the day's action, training, attack trials and formation riding. Gustav is excited by all the activity and is in no doubt that this is his future.

As he prepares his horse he does not notice Emma and a couple of girls preparing horses nearby.

For most of the morning Gustav and Henri ride hard over different ground conditions, including jumping ditches and numerous obstacles. Eventually Henri shouts, "race you back to the stables." Henri shows his skill and experience by racing far ahead. Gustav in his determination misjudges a jump and is pitched out of his saddle, landing heavily on the ground, which, fortunately is soft and muddy. He is, however, badly winded. Henri continues at speed, not noticing Gustav's fall. Emma and her friends, riding nearby, see his fall.

Emma rides quickly over to Gustav, leaps off her horse and crouches down beside him. As she reaches to remove mud from his eyes, she anxiously enquires," how are you feeling?"

Gustav, still a bit winded, coughs and splutters shakily says, "I think I am alright." Then he realises that here is an opportunity to get close to Emma, so he groans loudly. Emma takes him in her arms. He is overwhelmed by her presence. Emma is not fooled as she sees the twinkle in his eye and is intrigued by it. The spell is broken by the arrival of Henri. Emma releases Gustav and returns to her friends, who are waiting nearby while Henri helps him to his feet.

Henri sees that Gustav is uninjured and helps him back on his horse. "Oh, dear, you are a naughty lad. Did you fall off the horse deliberately, I wonder?" Gustav smiles broadly, replying, "maybe."

As they set off back to the stables Gustav waves to Emma, shouting, "thank you. See you again soon, I hope."

Back at the stables, while Gustav is caring for his horse, Emma appears at his side saying, "I just thought that I would see if you weren't badly hurt." Gustav is dazzled by her impish smile and throwing all caution to the wind, takes her in his arms, whispering, "thank you for caring." Emma does not resist as she is caught up in the magic of the moment. As she breaks away she breathes, "we must be careful as Duke William is jealous of my welfare."

"I do not care. I must see you again. Can we meet here from time to time? I think that if I prove worthy of joining the cavalry, and you want to be with me I could persuade the Duke to allow me to court you. Maybe your father would help if I proved to him that I would care for you."

Emma agrees and then leaves the stables without making any arrangement to meet again. She is thinking that, at first, meetings could appear to be accidental, since she will be riding with friends frequently.

It does not take long for Henri to believe that Gustav has talent and that he learns quickly. He reports this to Duke William who summons Gustav to an audience. There Duke William announces, "Gustav, Henri has reported that you have talent for horse-riding and leadership. I have, therefore, decided that you will join my cavalry for further training. There are momentous military events planned for the near future and I'd like you, together with some others, to be part of them. If you do well I will reward you handsomely. In the meantime, I will provide you with a horse and all the necessary equipment. Mind you care for them properly."

Gustav bows deeply, "I shall be worthy of your trust."

"You had better be," says Duke William as he dismisses him.

Gustav feels that he has achieved his vocation and has the opportunity to make a name for himself. While he is aware that the prophesy of the Norse Gods has started to be fulfilled he has no idea how things will develop.

"I will simply follow my fortunes and see where they lead," he thinks.

Meantime, he cannot stop thinking of Emma.

CHAPTER TWENTY-FOUR

GUSTAV GRADUATES

Along with a small group of promising cavalry colleagues undergoing training in complex manoeuvres, cavalry control disciplines and horsemanship, Gustav is enjoying the fellowship of his colleagues.

The training includes mock battles against experienced cavalry and infantry formations during which Gustav is showing extraordinary ability. His trainers mark him out for special attention and also set situations where his leadership skills can be identified and developed.

Whenever possible he meets Emma at the stables. One day they decide they must meet somewhere private and on an afternoon when Gustav is free he asks Emma, "would you ride out to the valley and explore it and the river with me?"

"That's an interesting thought, why not," she replies coyly.

That afternoon, in glorious spring weather, they ride out openly together as they now realise that there is no point in their hiding their affection for each other. Of course, many people at the stables take note but no one is inclined to comment. Soon they are riding fast through the scrubland beyond the stables. Emma's long blond hair is flying out behind her enchanting Gustav who is having difficulty in keeping up. On reaching the valley they slow down and trot the horses to the river to drink. The scene is idyllic; the sun is shining in a cloudless sky, the birds are singing, and a light breeze ruffles the long grass. A short distance away there is a little patch of grass surrounded by low trees. Emma, laughing gaily takes Gustav's hand and pulls over to it. Gustav takes the horses' reins and tethers them to a sturdy tree so that they can graze the long succulent grass. They sit down close together and chatter.

Gustav has a strange feeling of déjà vu. He thinks that he has been here before but cannot see any detail. He shakes off the feeling to pay attention to Emma.

As she is talking Gustav cannot take his eyes off her and is absorbed in her personality. He thinks, "I want the girl to be with me for ever." Emma stops chattering, senses what Gustav is thinking but cannot resist asking, "what are you thinking about? You seem so far away."

"Emma," he replies shakily, "I love you to so much, please come here." He holds his arms out and Emma rolls over to him in floods of tears.

"I love you too." They hold each other and then kiss slowly then passionately. Shortly after Emma pulls away wearing a troubled expression and through her tears says, "what are we to do?"

Gustav, displaying a confidence he actually does not have, says, "We speak to your father and mother first to gain their approval and when we get that we should be able to persuade your father to have a word with Duke William. I cannot see why the Duke should object as I am sure I have a commanding future in the cavalry."

Emma agrees, saying," let's discuss how we are going to do this." They eventually agree that the best plan is for them both to get together with Emma's parents and take it from there. They think it wise, however, that Emma has a word with her mother in advance to prepare the ground.

They stay a little while longer telling each other of their backgrounds and then return jauntily to the stables. As they leave, Gustav again has this feeling of having been in this situation before. Unbeknown to Gustav, Goddess Freya is quietly watching…

A week later as Gustav has just finished a gruelling mock combat exercise, Emma comes to him in a very excited frame of mind, "Gustav, I have spoken to mother and she has agreed that you should come to visit and eat with us tomorrow, if you are free.

She has mentioned us to father who is agreeable to your eating with us."

Gustav responds," excellent, I will be there." Gustav is thinking that he would be rejected.

All next day both Gustav and Emma are excited. Gustav makes a serious mistake during manoeuvres through not paying attention and is criticised by his commander. Emma cannot concentrate on anything, much to the amusement of her friends, who are curious as to what is happening. They are all aware of Emma's feelings for Gustav.

As Emma has told him where she lives, he walks to her house which is a substantial building, indicating the great wealth of its owner. Trying not to be intimidated, he knocks on the door which is immediately opened by Emma who must have been standing just behind it.

She leads him to a large beautifully furnished room where her parents are waiting. Emma introduces him to them. He is immediately at ease as the welcome is warm and genuine, especially as Emma stands close to him. Her parents are in no doubt of Emma's feelings.

They go through to another room where servants are ready to serve the meal. The meal progresses during which conversation is light-hearted. and Afterwards they move back the reception room. Emma's father opens the serious conversation by saying, "mother has told me that you wish permission to court, not only from us, but also from Duke William. Gustav, I have made enquiries about you and I am told that you are training to be a cavalry officer. This is a prestigious occupation and as far as I am concerned I give you our blessing. I am in council with Duke William next week when I shall plead your case. Pending his decision, you must avoid meeting, as rumour of clandestine meetings will prejudice your case."

Mother adds, "I am happy to receive you Gustav at any time, but you must, please, be patient."

Father says, with a serious expression on his face, "I must warn you not to breach our conditions. If you do, you will anger Duke William and that is very unwise."

Gustav and Emma agree and then the family enjoy an evening of gossip and exchanging details of each family's background.

Gustav leaves the house in good spirits after having given Emma a warm embrace.

Duke William holds his Council meeting at the end of which Robert seeks an audience which is granted. Robert tells Duke William of the wish for Gustav and Emma to court. Duke William answers," Ah yes, I remember that young man. On a recommendation I summoned him to meet me. I was impressed and allowed him to join my cavalry for training and evaluation. I am hearing good reports of him. I have no objection to their courting, but I will not sanction a marriage unless and until Gustav is fit to stay in the cavalry as a commander. It is likely for this to take a year or so."

Robert replies to the Duke, "thank you sir, I accept the conditions and I will ensure they are adhered to."

Robert returns home to tell Emma the good news who immediately rushes out to meet Gustav.

Gustav, as if he needed it, now has a powerful incentive to excel in his training.

During the next year Gustav trains hard, earning the praise and respect of his trainers. During a brutal combat training exercise Gustav and his team find themselves in serious difficulties which are not part of the training plan. Gustav, seeing the danger, shouts out, "wheel left NOW and charge." His companions react immediately thereby avoiding serious injury.

Back at camp Gustav's quick thinking is praised by all and Henri decides to report that the time has come for Gustav to graduate as a commander, with Duke William's approval.

He meets Duke William as the Duke is resting after a successful day's hunting, The Duke has listened to Henri's reports and decides that Gustav should be appointed a commander. The Duke invites Gustav to join him. He tells him," you have justified my faith in you, and I will confirm your appointment at a special banquet at the castle next week for all my cavalry commanders. Only when you are appointed will I agree that you may marry my cousin Emma. Just make sure you keep her happy, because if you do not you will answer to me!"

"Thank you, sir, for your decision and your permission to marry Emma. I look forward to serving you."

Afterwards Gustav goes to Emma's house to give her the good news. There is great joy in the house and after the evening meal Emma and Gustav go for a long walk arm in arm, laughing and joking, until Emma becomes serious, saying," we must be serious as I know we will be apart for long periods of time as you go campaigning with Duke William during which you will be in great danger!"

At the banquet the following week, and just before the serious drinking starts, Duke William calls for order.

"Gentlemen, it is my pleasure to command Gustav to my presence now to receive his spurs on his acceptance into my elite cavalry. Gustav, to me please."

Gustav moves forward to the dais and top table amid cheers from his fellow cavalry men. Gustav bows to Duke William who presents him with his spurs. "Serve me well Gustav. I place great trust in you. During tomorrow you will receive your horse and be fitted with your armour. Treat them well."

The Duke extends his hand and Gustav bows to kiss the ring amid roars of congratulation from all present.

With lots of back slapping and good-natured banter he returns to his table knowing that he will have to earn those spurs. He also knows that there will be plenty of opportunity as the Duke is still having to meet and defeat those who would challenge his supremacy.

He is allowed one night out of barracks and spends the time with Emma until the early hours before going to his house. Emma is worried about his safety and she whispers to him," I love you so much that I will always worry for your safety. However, I want you to do well."

Gustav replies, "thank you for your loving concern. I feel the same about you." I am off to Harfleur tomorrow as William wants to deal with a few troublemakers. I may see my first action. When I get back I will then ask your parents and Duke William to allow us to fix a date for our wedding."

Duke William sets off early next morning with a force of five hundred comprising three hundred infantry, one hundred archers and one hundred cavalry. Rumour has it that another minor magnate is moving out to the region of Evereux, an action that provokes William's anger. There follows a series of fierce skirmishes at the end of which William prevails and receives the homage of the defeated magnate.

Gustav proves to be less effective as a cavalry leader and becomes aware that he has much to learn from actual combat conditions. Duke William is not impressed either and makes his feelings known.

"You will have to do better if you are to be worthy of the trust I place in you," says the Duke with a scowl on his face.

On the return journey to Caen they are ambushed by a large group of invaders from Maine. During heavy fighting ensues Gustav sees an opportunity. Calling his cavalry together he yells," follow me!"

Gustav gallops off as though fleeing the battlefield. Duke William sees this and angrily assumes Gustav is pulling out of the battle. In reality Gustav leads his horsemen in a wide circle behind rising ground, falls upon the enemy's rear and decimates their infantry. The enemy collapse and flee hotly pursued by the cavalry, inflicting heavy losses upon them. At the end of the day William calls Gustav to him, saying, "that was a brilliant manoeuvre. Well done. You have atoned for your earlier failure. I plan that we return to Falaise to regroup. I will give you three weeks leave to marry Emma and settle to create a family!"

Gustav's companions laugh noisily with many ribald jokes as the army returns to Falaise.

CHAPTER TWENTY-FIVE

GUSTAV MARRIES

Gustav continues on to Caen, after having obtained Duke William's agreement to attend the wedding.

Gustav rides fast into Caen, arriving at Emma's house in a state of great excitement, finding Emma coming out of the door. He leaps off his horse, embraces her saying, "Duke William has given us leave to get married, but we must marry now because I have three weeks before I have to return to base! Have we time?"

Emma steps back and says, "Oh yes, Mother and I have everything planned: all we have to do is inform the guests and the priest of the date. A week's notice is enough as father is experienced in the ways of Duke William and the army.

Gustav is concerned, saying," I asked Duke William to be a guest and he agreed to come. I doubt there is sufficient notice."

Chortling, Emma says, "Father will send a messenger as soon as we confirm the date. He will come as I am his favourite cousin!

Gustav then goes, with Emma, to the family house where Olaf and Iona are still living. They are received with great excitement, and during a fine meal prepared by Iona, Gustav tells of his adventures since they were last together. Afterwards, Olaf and Iona tell of what they have been doing.

Iona explains, "I am being courted by a local farmer's son. His mother died long ago, and his father does not have long to live. David will inherit the farm and then we shall marry."

Gustav and Emma are delighted, Gustav exclaiming," I hope I can get back from campaign for your wedding!"

They listen to Emma and Gustav explaining their wedding arrangements to everyone's delight.

On a more serious note they discuss living arrangements as the house is too small to accommodate everybody.

They agree that the house be extended immediately as there is plenty of land. While it is understood that Iona will move to her husband's farm after her marriage, it is agreed that Emma and her family will live in the extended part of the house with, Olaf retaining the original part of the building. Pending completion of the extension Emma will continue to live with her parents. Gustav, counselling caution, explains that there can be no certainty that he and Emma can settle in Caen. In a spirit of harmony, they agree to the plan and to share the cost as extra space will always be useful.

Gustav draws attention to the matter of Freya's brooch," as we all know the care of the brooch is through the wife of the first-born son. We also know of its special powers of protection of the owners, and that the whole family is protected at all times into the future."

"When Emma and I are married the brooch will be given to Emma and its safety becomes the responsibility of her and her successors into the future as required by our mother."

Olaf and Iona immediately accept this with Emma saying, "I am honoured and promise that I will take great care of it and ensure that its purpose is explained to each future generation."

The date for the wedding is set ten days hence and all the guests are immediately advised. This is not a problem as they all live in, or near to, Caen. A messenger is sent to Duke William who immediately confirms he will be there. Accommodation is quickly organised in Caen castle for the Duke and his retainers.

The wedding is a grand affair with much feasting and dancing held in the great square in front of the keep in Caen castle. For early spring, the weather is kind. There are only two speeches, one from Duke William wishing the couple well and the other from Gustav ceremoniously handing over Freya's brooch, exclaiming loudly so that all the guests can hear, "Emma, please take custody of our mother's brooch as is required by our original faith in the Nordic Gods. Guard it well and ensure it is passed down with an explanation of its origin and purpose to future generations."

The Christian priest is less than impressed by this. Olaf whispers in his ear," keep your counsel, there is nothing you can say that is helpful. The Nordic Gods will continue to influence our family's fortunes covertly." The priest stays quiet in the face of such palpable menace.

At the height of the festivities Emma and Gustav slip away, after telling Duke William, "we are slipping away to a very private place, revered by Gustav's parents, for a little while."

Duke William laughs somewhat coarsely, "use the time wisely!"

Before the wedding Gustav had explained to Emma the significance of the glade by the river and its importance in ensuring that Goddess Freya is worshipped.

The quietly leave the festivities and walk happily hand in hand to the glade. Strangely, there is no-one there. As with Freya and Frode the scene is tranquil with a very light breeze rustling the new spring leaves on the trees.

They kneel together and, holding hands, pray, "Goddess Freya we give you our lives to protect our family through the brooch Emma is now wearing. We pray to you that our union will be fruitful and is worthy of the power and influence our family acquire."

Once again the glade is suffused with warm light and the couple sense that Goddess Freya has blessed them.

After a little while they leave the glade and return to the festivities.

As with all Viking Norman weddings the festivities are raucous, and revelry goes on well into the night. Gustav and Emma retire to the family house warm in the knowledge that they are ready to go wherever their lives take them.

Later in the morning, amid guests suffering from sore heads, Duke William calls all together and announces," it has been a pleasure to share this wedding with you. I wish you all well as I leave you to continue my campaign to make Normandy great."

CHAPTER TWENTY-SIX

DUKE WILLIAM SUBDUES ALL OPPOSITION

A year after the wedding Emma gives birth to a son, who they call Richard. The extension to the family house is completed and after Richard is born Emma moves in as agreed.

Gustav is heavily engaged in Duke William's battles to gain the ascendancy over all opposition in Normandy which has taken nearly twenty years. He has established himself as a brave and resourceful cavalryman and he is soon appointed Duke William's Commander of Cavalry.

Despite the frequency of military action, Gustav is able to return to his family in Caen quite often. He and Emma have a second son called Roald. Later they have three daughters.

Emma spends time helping Olaf and his partners in the trading business, while bringing up the children.

Gustav is appointed to Duke William's council of knights, honours him by naming him Robert of Normandy and Count of Mortain, the original Count having been killed in a skirmish some years before.

Duke William wins major battles against King Henry 1st of France. In the second decisive battle, Gustav, now known as Robert, leads the cavalry into a crushing attack on the French infantry. The skirmishes in areas such as Maine cease as Duke William reigns supreme leading to a period of relative peace.

Shortly afterwards Duke William meets with Edward the Confessor, King of England. During that meeting Duke William is convinced that Edward, having no children, nominates him as his successor, William being Edward's cousin. Unfortunately, there were no witnesses, nor is there any written record. Duke William uses the relative quiet to build up his fleet, initially as a defence. He soon understands that he may have to use his fleet in an offensive role.

His spies in England inform him that Edward is in the thrall of the powerful Godwain family. They appear to have a stronger claim to the throne, but William is not one to be put off once he decides on a course of action. He covets the crown of England.

King Edward dies and the crown is taken over by Harold Godwain. William is not best pleased and decides that he must claim the throne by force of arms. His decision to expand his navy is now vindicated.

He calls his Council of Knights to a meeting. When all are gathered in the castle of Falaise he announces, "the King of England is dead, and he nominated me his successor. The crown has been usurped by Harold Godwain. I want it, and I intend that we invade England to get it"

He continues, "we shall plan an invasion now, the winter storms will prevent our crossing to England before long. Go now, all of you, and come back in a week with ideas.

Duke William sends emissaries to other parts of France, Germany and Denmark offering great rewards to men willing to join his army.

In the meantime, the Council of Knights meets and offer their views. They receive reports from spies on suitable landing sites. There is much debate and eventually a site near Hastings is decided on. Embarkation at Cherbourg is agreed. About half of the invasion army of over seven thousand men are mercenaries. The army assembles near Cherbourg, comprising infantry, archers, and his fearsome cavalry, commanded by Robert of Normandy.

Word reaches Duke William that King Harold is with his army in the north of England fighting a Viking invasion. There is not a moment to lose, so Duke William increases his demand for faster assembly. Even this takes a couple of weeks before the army is complete. He has to wait for the sea conditions for the crossing to England to be calm enough.

CHAPTER TWENTY-SEVEN

DUKE WILLIAM INVADES ENGLAND

The invasion force sets off in ideal sea conditions, there being just a gentle swell and light winds. The visibility is excellent under a clear blue sky. Duke William believes his fervent prayers prior to embarkation have been heard and answered. The men are in high spirits and are looking forward to gaining great wealth from the spoils of war.

The crossing is uneventful, although Robert is seasick and needs attention from his second in command.

The fleet makes landfall on a shingle beach at Pevensey and meets no opposition. Most men are employed in forming a bridgehead, while some go inland as raiding parties. It takes several days to build shelters and build the defensive earthworks.

Meantime, Harold, who has just inflicted a heavy defeat on the Viking forces at Stamford Bridge in the north, hears of Duke William's landing. He quickly gathers his depleted forces and marches rapidly south, collecting strong reinforcements on the way, particularly in and around London.

Harold then marches fast westwards hoping to catch the Normans off guard, but Duke William's scouts see his army just in time. However, The

Normans fail to secure the high ground overlooking the bay and the Saxon army is able to seize and hold this area, establishing an almost impenetrable shield wall.

The battle starts well after sunrise by the Norman forces charging uphill at the shield wall. For many hours, the shield wall holds even against the continuing storms of arrows falling upon King Harold's men.

With the Normans suffering grievous losses achieving little, Duke William calls a halt and brings his commanders together for consultations.

Robert speaks, "Sir, do you remember your idea during a battle a couple of years ago when you ordered me to withdraw the cavalry as though we were retreating? We then pounced on the enemy who had chased after us,"

Robert cleverly ascribes his plan to William!

Duke William smiles broadly, "my view precisely. Gather round everybody while I explain how we are going to do this. There will be two trumpet calls to signal the cavalry's apparent fleeing the field and the infantry drawing back. Assuming the Saxons rush down chasing us there will be three trumpet calls when our forces will turn to envelope the fools."

"Go to it!"

The ploy is not wholly successful. During the manoeuvre not all of the Saxon infantry stream down the hill in pursuit of the retreating Normans, in defiance of orders from their commanders, who see the dangers. Suddenly, a cry goes up from the Saxons, "the king is dead." He has been struck in the head by an arrow, causing the Saxon forces hesitate. Three Norman trumpet calls blare out above the noise and the Normans turn and, led by Robert's cavalry, charge up the hill, breach the shield wall causing the Saxon forces to break and flee.

Within the hour the Normans are triumphant.

The remaining hours of daylight are spent by regrouping, retrieving the dead and finding King Harold's body.

Robert assembles his cavalry, "I salute you all. You have made history this day and you will all share in the spoils of victory. I will ensure that Duke William recognises your greatness. Retire now and rest. We shall see later what we are to do next."

Duke William gathers his commanders saying, "I acknowledge our men's bravery. Let us give thanks to God and offer prayers for the souls of those Normans who have died today"

Robert quietly offers a prayer of thanks to Goddess Freya, asking, once again that she watches over Emma and the children in Normandy.

Duke William calls another council of war to agree the next phase of the invasion.

He addresses the assembled body, "we must strike fast to exploit the confusion after the battle. I will take a force to head along the coast to take Dover and Canterbury and then move on London. Another will strike north to take Winchester and seize the treasury, moving then to join me in London taking Reading on the way. Finally, I want a small force to be detached at Winchester after submissions have been received. They are to subdue Devon and Cornwall."

He continues, "I believe that a large part of King Harold's army lies in the north and we must be ready to deal with them if we have to."

Standing tall he confidently claims," England is ours. Let's take over London where I shall be crowned king. Then I shall summons all the earls and other Saxon leaders to my presence to swear fealty to me. I intend to appoint a full Norman hierarchy as soon as possible, rewarding all of you who have made my claim to the English throne a reality."

Robert is instructed to take the detachment of cavalry to Winchester to seize King Harold's treasury and thereafter to make for London with it. He sends the force to Devon and Cornwall, led by his second in command.

All the actions are carried out swiftly and ruthlessly.

Less than a month after the battle, William has control of the south of England and London. Robert delivers the submissions of Saxon earls and hands over the Saxon treasury to William. On Christmas Day William is crowned king. He sends messengers to the counties north of London summonsing Saxon earls to come to him in London to submit to his authority. As not all do so, King William has to enforce their submission, sending Robert's cavalry as his demonstration of power.

Meantime, many members of the Norman aristocracy come to England looking for grants of land. King William is in no hurry to make such grants, wanting to ensure that claimants are genuine.

In a fierce skirmish fifty miles north of London, Robert is unhorsed and lands heavily. His arm is injured badly, so much so, that he loses the use of it. He is led to London where he reports to King William who realises that Robert is no longer fit to remain in the army.

King William calls a meeting of all his councillors. With full pomp and ceremony, he announces. "I have before us Robert of Normandy, Count of Mortain. He has sustained injury serving us bravely in battle. Sadly, he is no longer able to command my cavalry. In recognition of his service to us I discharge him from his duties and grant to him, all the lands held by the Saxon King Harold in Cornwall, to be held by him and his successors in perpetuity, giving fealty to Cadoc, who I have appointed Earl of Cornwall.

In creating him Baron Robert of Bodmin in Cornwall, I grant to him all mineral and all fishing rights in Cornwall subject to the payment of fees to the Crown through Earl Cadoc together with knights as I require for my army. I shall have to determine these later when my kingdom is settled.

In addition, I grant him twenty mounted retainers and a sum of money to help him establish control over his lands in Cornwall."

The announcement is received with wide acclaim, many seeing this as the beginning of land grants being made.

Robert kneels, saying, "my Lord King, I pledge fealty to you and to Earl Cadoc, for the grant of these lands."

King William dismisses them and turns his attention to other business.

CHAPTER TWENTY-EIGHT

ROBERT OCCUPIES HIS LANDS IN CORNWALL

Robert spends several weeks in London preparing to travel to Cornwall. The grant of land comprises over fifty per cent of Cornwall's area. He has to arrange to protect the large sum of money granted by King William. While this is happening, he sends envoys to Earl Cadoc carrying King William's Charter granting the lands and the other rights to Robert.

Just prior to Robert's departure he receives a message from Cadoc acknowledging his grant and his fealty.

Baron Robert and his entourage take a month to reach Cornwall. On the way they reinforce the overlordship of King William with the people they meet on the way.

As they near Cornwall Robert sends an envoy ahead to meet Earl Cadoc and to arrange a meeting at the border between Cornwall and Wessex. Robert is concerned to work out how he can exercise his rights over land that has not been granted to him. When he raised the point with King William the king waved his hand and had said, "oh, sort it out with Earl Cadoc!"

At the border meeting, after confirmation of fealty, Earl Cadoc tells Robert, "I have arranged for you to occupy a large manor house at Bodmin. There is accommodation for you and your retainers pending your decision to remain there or to extend it. Meantime you are my guests at Tremanton where I hope to build a castle. In a few days I shall escort you to Bodmin."

Robert responds with a small bow. "thank you for your welcome and guidance. I suggest, when I am established in Bodmin, we meet again to agree our respective roles and other administrative matters. I wish to bring my wife and family over immediately."

Cadoc, smiling, "yes, I am sure you have missed them. I hope that all turns out well."

Two days later Robert sets off to cover the twenty-five or so miles to Bodmin accompanied by his entourage and an escort led by Earl Cadoc.

The journey proves uneventful as the locals are quiet. Earl Cadoc suggests that the Cornish people were not too impressed by the Saxon kings and tended to get on with their lives regardless.

On arrival Robert finds the manor and its outbuildings in good habitable condition and over the following weeks everybody settles in. Robert sets off for Caen to reunite with Emma, Richard, Roald and the three girls and then to bring them to Bodmin. The reunion is boisterous. After passionate embraces and exchanging news of events which had taken place since they were last together,

Robert helps Emma gather their belongings ready to move to England. Richard and Roald are very excited, but the girls are unhappy about leaving their friends.

Robert and Emma spend time visiting friends making farewells.

Just before they leave, Robert and Olaf discuss plans for the future. Robert explains," Olaf, Cornwall is rich in tin which is highly sought after. I plan to extend existing mines and open new ones. I need to expand, and I thought you could support me there, with your ships moving the tin from Cornwall."

Olaf, seeing a chance to expand his trading influence, "I agree. Let me know when you have settled down and I will come to Cornwall to agree how we are going to do it."

Robert returns to Cornwall with Emma and the children in a ship provided by Olaf. Olaf has ordered the captain and senior officers to land at

Fowey, staying for a few weeks exploring to see if trading markets can be set up in addition to trading in tin.

Robert has a further meeting with Earl Cadoc in which Robert receives a free hand in developing tin mining and other commercial interests in return for an annual fee to the Crown and to him, the amount to be agreed later.

During the next ten years Robert tours his lands extensively, arranging expansion of tin mining and opening new mines through a team of experts, some of whom come from Normandy. The trading between the two families in Cornwall and Normandy grows greatly.

By this time Robert is ageing and decides to start passing control to his oldest son, Richard who has been training under his father.

Richard marries a Cornish girl, Senara. Emma shows her the brooch which she will inherit When doing so Emma explains the brooch's history, its powers, and the rule of its bequest in future years. Afterwards Senara, although a Christian, is persuaded to join with Emma in a prayer of understanding and commitment to Goddess Freya.

Shortly after the wedding Richard and Senara start tobuild a substantial house not far from the family manor and start raising a family.

Richard's brother, Roald is not really interested in the mining business and devotes his time to raising flocks of sheep throughout the county, working through a team of skilful and dedicated shepherds.

The amount of wool produced is substantial with it being exported to Normandy through using the trading family's business. The wool is prepared for export and loaded onto Olaf's ships at Fowey. The wealth generated is used to invest in opening new tin mines.

King William issues a summons for Roald to go to London to serve in his Court. The King is concerned to ensure that Cornwall does not become too powerful and tacitly holds Roald as a hostage.

King William soon discovers that Roald has organisational skills and appoints him to coordinate the work of the assessors who are gathering information for the production of the Domesday Book. On completion of the work King William shows his gratitude by granting Roald a large part of Suffolk together with the title of Baron Roald of Suffolk, allowing him and his descendants to build a wool export business and later to be major farmers.

During the same period Olaf marries in Normandy and continues to build a successful business which extends to the Mediterranean and the Ottoman Empire. In addition, he maintains trade with England through his brother and nephews.

The solid foundation for the development of the dynasty has been established in Norman England, France, the Mediterranean and the Near East.

The family moves into the future, holding high offices of state, creating industrial empires, with each generation producing a master storyteller. It is always guarded by

Goddess Freya through the powers vested in Frode's brooch.

Over the centuries the family loses the memory of their Viking heritage despite the existence of the brooch whose significance is also lost.

Goddess Freya, deeply concerned about this, decides to devise a means of reminding the family. She decides that she should appear before a skilled storyteller descendant in a vision to task him with creating the story of the family and the prophesy from which it was created.

It takes her many years for her to find him…

EPILOGUE

THE FRADDON FESTIVAL OF CORNISH FOLKLORE

Tristan now considers the presentation he wishes to make to the Fraddon Festival. He has tested his ideas with audiences at Fowey harbour and then writes up the material suitable for an audience having an expectation of a rousing story.

Goddess Freya has watched over his preparations and believes Tristan will ensure the Viking foundation will not ever be forgotten.

As the audience settles down the Master of Ceremonies announces, "ladies and gentlemen. We are now to hear a story from our own Tristan Penhaligan, called "The Viking and the Lady."

To a roar of applause Tristan walks to the centre of the area carrying a large model of a Viking longship, followed by a friend carrying a table upon which Tristan places the model.

Tristan raises his hands high; the audience quietens.

Tristan, in a strong vibrant voice carrying to all parts of the amphitheatre speaks.

"Ladies and Gentlemen. Over a thousand years ago…"

Printed in Great Britain
by Amazon